MW01257060

## CONTENTS

# CORGI CASE FILES

## CASE OF THE

# SHADY SHAMROCK

Book 12

# J.M. POOLE

Secret Staircase Books

Case of the Shady Shamrock
Published by Secret Staircase Books, an imprint of
Columbine Publishing Group, LLC
PO Box 416, Angel Fire, NM 87710

Book layout and design by Secret Staircase Books
Cover image © Felipe de Barros

First trade paperback edition: February, 2021
First e-book edition: February, 2021

* * *

**Publisher's Cataloging-in-Publication Data**

Poole, J.M.
Case of the Shady Shamrock / by J.M. Poole.
p. cm.
ISBN 978-1649140494 (paperback)
ISBN 978-1649140500 (e-book)

1. Zachary Anderson (Fictitious character)--Fiction. 2.
Pomme Valley, Oregon (fictitious location)—Fiction. 3. Amateur
sleuth—Fiction. 4. Pet detectives—Fiction. I. Title

Corgi Case Files Mystery Series : Book 12.
Poole, J.M., Corgi Case Files mysteries.

BISAC : FICTION / Mystery & Detective.

813/.54

# CORGI CASE FILES

Case of the
Shady Shamrock

Corgi Case Files, Book 12

By

J.M. Poole

**Sign up for Jeffrey's newsletter to get all the latest
corgi news—
Click here AuthorJMPoole.com**

## ACKNOWLEDGMENTS

Many thanks to my "discovery" of the NaNoWriMo challenge five years ago. Without it, I don't know if I would have ever started the Corgi Case Files series. For those of you who don't know about NaNoWriMo, it stands for 'National Novel Writing Month', where authors challenge themselves to write a 50,000 word story in a month's time. I didn't make it the first time I tried, for CCF1, but for the four following years, including this one, I've kicked its ever-lovin' butt! Yes, you can quote me on that.

The Irish Crown Jewels are, in fact, a real thing and, as you'll soon learn, *were* stolen in 1907. To this day, they have never been recovered, so ... I had some fun with that. Why not let a couple of inquisitive corgis try to work their magic on the case?

As always, I am incredibly grateful for the help of my dedicated group of family, readers, and friends for helping out with this novel. Diane, Caryl, Jason, Louise, Elizabeth, and Carol. I appreciate the support and, as you will no doubt attest, I definitely need it. :)

I'd also like to thank my new publisher's set of beta readers: Marcia Koopmann, Sandra Anderson, Paula Webb, and Susan Gross, who have been instrumental in catching every last grammar and punctuation error or typo in each manuscript as they've been re-released, and making them as flawless as we can. Thank you for all your time and effort, it's so appreciated!

Finally, I have to thank my readers and fans. This marks the 12th book of the series. I never would have imagined I'd get this far, and to be honest, the end is nowhere in sight. The next two titles have been announced, and will be released later this year.

Happy reading!

*For Giliane -*

*We had a magical time in Ireland. So much so that
I'm eager for more. When are we going back?*

# ONE

A re you absolutely sure you want to try that one? I'd think twice, if I were you."

"You did say that I could sample a few dishes before this event, didn't you? I realize people are still setting up, but you did say no one would get mad at me for sneaking a few morsels here and there, right?"

"Er, mad? No. I'm just thinking about your, er, digestive system."

My hand froze in mid-stretch, with my fork mere inches away from securing a four-inch-long segment of a dark, delicious-looking piece of sausage. Of all the various dishes at my disposal, this one actually smelled and looked the most appetizing. A quick check of the majority of the other dishes revealed a common denominator: a green substance I *loathed*. Who would've known the Irish eat so much cabbage? Cooked or raw, I couldn't stand it. That's why I thought my selection of a meat dish should've been my safest bet. Skeptically, I turned to my companion.

"What's wrong with it? It *is* sausage, isn't it? I mean, it looks like it, and smells like it, so I think it's safe to give it a try."

"It isn't sausage," Jillian Cooper, owner of Cookbook Nook, and my fiancée, clarified, with a remarkably straight face. "If you want to get technical, it's black pudding."

"Pudding?" I repeated. "Oh, I get it. Is that what the Irish call sausage?"

"In this case, yes."

I narrowed my eyes as I studied the piece of meat. Looking at the cross-section of the dish, I could see that the insides looked just as I expected, containing tiny pieces of fat, flecks of grain, and bits of spices interspersed throughout an otherwise darker-colored substance. I could easily see where it got its name, since the casing on this sausage was nearly black. Wait a minute. I *do* seem to recall being warned off from certain dishes when I visited the Emerald Isle a number of years ago. Was this one of them?

"You told me you've been to Ireland," Jillian said, smiling. "I know you can be a picky eater. How did you ever survive there? More to the point, you didn't actually eat this, did you?"

"My publisher warned me about certain dishes," I admitted. "Black pudding. I think you're right. I think this was one of them, only I don't remember why."

"Blood," Jillian answered.

"Blood? What about it?"

Jillian pointed at the plump coils of sausage. "The black part of the pudding refers to blood. This dish is made with pork blood and pork fat, or beef suet, and … Zachary? Are you all right? You're turning green."

While we wait for me and my stomach to return to speaking terms, perhaps I should introduce myself. My name is Zachary Anderson. I'm a writer, winery owner, police consultant, dog owner, and with regards to cuisine, culinary-impaired. I guess I should explain, so let's go through each of those.

First off, I'm a writer. No, my chosen genre isn't mystery, or fantasy, or anything else you would expect me to say. As it happens, I'm a romance writer, responsible for dozens of novels with scantily clad people on the covers. If you really want to be honest, the covers that sell the most copies for me are those that show the most skin, while keeping the proper, er, *bits* covered. I should also point out that you won't find my name on any book, but my nom de plume: Chastity Wadsworth. When I'm behind a computer, I let my fans and readers think I'm a woman. It's why my books sell so well. It's also why I obviously don't do any book-signings. Having written so many books, for so long, I've built up quite a devoted group of fans, and those readers are responsible for paying the bills.

No, wait. That's not all true. As I mentioned before, I hold a number of jobs. Let's move to the second, which is winery owner. This particular title requires me to do the absolute least, because I have a master vintner overseeing all stages of my wines' production. Caden Burne has been Lentari Cellars' self-proclaimed winemaster for the past couple of years, and I couldn't be happier. The only thing I have to do is sign checks. He tells me what I need to buy, and as long as there isn't a comma in the price tag, then I'll usually do it without any arguments.

For the record, if the price of the item Caden needs happens to be four figures, then he'll usually sit down with me and plead his case. Come to think of it, I haven't turned him down yet, and that's because I trust him implicitly with my winery. Whatever Caden needs, Caden gets.

Next up on my list of professions takes a little bit of explaining. You see, I've been hired as a consultant for the Pomme Valley police department. Where's that, you ask? PV, as we locals like to call it, is in the southwestern area of Oregon. We're a small town of less than 5,000 people, situated between the communities of Grants Pass and Medford.

Our police department is small, with less than ten full-time officers. As for me, well, I'm usually called in whenever a crime has been committed that has the potential of stumping the officials. What that really means, though, is that I'm brought in whenever Detective Vance Samuelson gives me a call. Let me stop you right there, because I know what you're thinking. Vance doesn't really want my help with anything. He wants *theirs*.

Who am I talking about? That'd be my two dogs, Sherlock and Watson. They are Pembroke Welsh Corgis and, like their namesakes, are incredibly skilled at solving mysteries. Those two dogs have solved murder cases, located missing property, and have found people who have no desire to be found. I would also like to be able to tell you it's something I trained them to do, only we both know that'd be one doozy of a lie.

Sherlock and Watson have the ability to sniff out clues that, to an outside observer, would appear to have no bearing on the case whatsoever. However, each and every time they locate something, regardless of how bizarre, it's later proven that the clue has a direct connection to the case. I just wish I knew how they did it.

Whenever the dogs home in on something, which could be a bit of trash, or a fluttering leaf, or anything else you or I would instantly classify as insignificant, I would take a picture of it. Then, after I had taken enough 'corgi clues', my friends and I would sit down—usually over dinner—and try to figure them out. Have we ever figured out the case before the dogs? No. I have no idea how the corgis work their magic. The only thing I can tell you is that Sherlock and Watson are the police department's secret weapons. The only thing I am is official Kibble Acquirer and Poo Picker-upper.

Yes, those are technical terms.

In case you were wondering, their Royal Canineships were over at Vance's house playing with his girls, while I was able to have some quiet time with my aforementioned fiancée. Although, if I am to be truthful, this wasn't the quiet time I was expecting.

Jillian Cooper is the owner extraordinaire of Cookbook Nook, a specialty cookbook store located here, in PV. It's a well-known fact that Jillian loves to host events at her store, whether it's a store-wide promotion or a local cookbook author providing a demonstration of some recipes found in their cookbooks.

Jillian had asked me earlier in the day if I could help her set up tables and chairs for an event Cookbook Nook was hosting. Then, she uttered the magic words which would always guarantee I'd offer my help: free food. Let's just say I couldn't get to my Jeep fast enough. What I didn't know, however, was the nature of this particular event. Since we were in the second week of March, that could only mean this particular festival had something to do with the rapidly-approaching St. Patrick's Day.

Now, I don't know about the rest of you, but the only real observation I've done for this particular holiday was to have a beer or two. No, they weren't dyed green. I don't care how good the beer tastes, if it's green, then it stays in the bottle, thank you very much.

I didn't care for corned beef, and you may recall me expressing my utter dislike for cabbage. What did that leave me? Well, I know the Irish were fond of potatoes, so that usually meant hitting the drive-thru at McDonald's for an order or two of French Fries.

This particular year, though, was different. Jillian had decided she wanted to host an authentic céilí. Well, after I looked up the word online, I saw that it simply meant an Irish festival, with food, music, dancing, and storytelling. Since there was no way she'd be able to clear enough space for a dance floor, she had to settle for three of the four requirements.

Turns out Oregon has over 10% of its population tracing back to Ireland in some fashion. What did that mean for PV? Well, we have some older folk who were born and raised in Éire. I had to look up that word, too. Éire is Irish for Ireland. You'd think I would have known the word, having some faint Irish blood running through my veins and having spent time over in County Cork a few years back.

Having questionable taste buds (hence the culinary-impaired label I had branded myself with earlier), I ended up researching quite a few recipes before anything could come even *remotely* close to my mouth. However, after sampling the third or fourth recipe, and finding it harmless, I let my guard down. Serves me right, I guess.

"Will you try this one?" Jillian asked me, as she pointed at one of four 13"x9" pans of a white, fluffy substance.

"What is it? Mashed potatoes? Of course."

"Is that what you think it is?" Jillian asked, bemused.

About ready to scoop some of the 'potatoes' onto my plate, I let out a sigh.

"Fine. What is it? It sure looks like potatoes. Smells like them, too."

"The top layer *is* mashed potatoes," Jillian confirmed.

"And the bottom layer?" I hesitantly asked.

Jillian shrugged. "Well, there's ground meat, usually lamb, but in this case, it's beef, with brown gravy and ..."

"Shepherd's pie," I said, as I grinned and resumed scooping a helping onto my plate. "Finally, something I know, seeing how I've had it before."

"And you liked it?" Jillian asked, impressed.

"There's nothing in here that I don't like," I confidently reported, as I prepared for my first bite. Then, I caught sight of Jillian's face, which had a guarded expression on it. "There isn't, is there?"

Jillian broke out in laughter. "I'm just teasing you. I made that batch, and I can assure you it is Zachary-approved."

"Awesome. Oh, man. This is good, lady. I should

keep you around more often."

Jillian snuggled close. "You already do. And thank you. My family loves shepherd's pie. I've made quite a few of them."

"Is your family part Irish?"

"Not that I am aware of. My family is mostly Swedish."

"Swedish? How did I not know that?"

"I've never told you?" Jillian asked, surprised. "I'm sorry. I should have said something sooner."

"No worries. Have you ever been to Sweden?"

"No, but I'd like to."

"In that case," I decided, "we should plan a trip."

"How exciting!" Jillian exclaimed. "But, could I make a request?"

"Sure."

"Could we make it Ireland? I've listened to you talk about your visit, and I've heard others talk about theirs. I've always wanted to go."

I pretended to think. "Ireland? Seriously?"

"I know you prefer to visit new places every time you travel," Jillian began, mistaking my hesitation for reluctance, "but there are some places that do require a more thorough look, don't you think?"

"If we plan a trip to Ireland," I slowly began, as I tried to keep the smile from spreading across my face, "then that would make the second trip for you, and the third for me."

As expected, Jillian stared at me with confusion written across her lovely features.

"Huh? I don't know what that means. I haven't been there before."

"But we *are* going there for our honeymoon, aren't we?"

Jillian gasped with surprise. "We are? What …? When …? You're not playing some type of prank on me, are you?"

"We talked about this," I began, completely enjoying myself, "a few nights ago. It was while we were watching *Notting Hill 2 — The Reckoning.*"

"But … we watched that on Tuesday."

"That's right."

"And I … fell asleep."

"Yes, you did," I recalled, with a smile. "I just assumed you were okay with my decision, especially when there were no objections afterward."

Jillian swatted my arm. "Objections? I was asleep! And heavens no, there are no objections. Are we really going?"

"For our honeymoon, yep," I confirmed. "I was going to plan out the rest, but then I realized I wanted to get your opinion on a few things."

"This is so exciting!"

"Is this an acceptable time to talk about this?" I asked, as I looked around the tables at the people milling about.

"Absolutely. You can't bring up Ireland to me now and not expect me to inquire about our itinerary. What do you need help with?"

Jillian and I stepped over to an adjacent table.

On it were four different dishes in commercial buffet warmers. We stopped at the first dish and stared at the offerings.

"Well, I wanted to ask you ... well, first, I want to know what *that* is. Should I take one?"

"That's a boxty."

"A boxty? And that would be ...?"

"It's a potato pancake, made with mashed potatoes and grated potatoes."

"The Irish do love their potatoes," I quietly observed. "It also sounds harmless. I'll try one. Will you as well?"

Jillian held out her plate in response. After placing a boxty on each of our plates, we moved on.

"As I was saying," I continued, "with regard to spending a full two weeks in Ireland, I thought ..."

"Two weeks!" Jillian excitedly repeated. "Oh, this keeps getting better and better!"

"Two weeks," I confirmed. "The first time I visited Ireland, I can tell you I was part of a tour group. Everything was done for me. I went where I was told, when I was told, and was only able to see things that were nearby. The caveat to that is someone else did the planning. The only thing I had to do was show up. Now, I have since learned there are tons of things to see, and plenty to do, so my question to you is, would you want to explore the country on our own? Or would you prefer to go through a travel agency and have them arrange everything?"

"Oooo, that's a good question. Perhaps I could

come over tonight and we can go through a travel guide together? We could then each point out what's most important to us."

"You're on, m'lady," I drawled, using what I'm hoping was a passable John Wayne accent.

We made it to the next offering and I have to say that I was frowning long before I made it to the dish. What I was looking at was a huge punch-bowl-sized container, filled to the brim with mashed potatoes, and mixed throughout was some type of green ingredient. Parsley, perhaps? Although, if it was, then that was a whole heckuva lot of it, and what I was looking at was a lot lighter than parsley. My nose, on the other hand, told me whatever it was, it didn't appeal to me in the slightest.

"What's that frown for?" Jillian wanted to know. "This is a very popular dish in Ireland. It's colcannon."

"There's something about the smell," I quietly began, as I leaned away from the dish. "Let me guess. Those aren't potatoes, but mashed up turnips and root vegetables? I was faked out once a few years back. Wow, it didn't taste good. That, there, looks like ... you didn't make it, did you?"

Jillian laughed. "No."

"Okay, good. I have to know. Does that smell like something you'd like to try?"

"I think it smells fine, but then again, I do enjoy cooked cabbage."

I leaned forward to peer into the depths of the

large container of colcannon. "Is *that* what I'm smelling? Cooked cabbage?"

"It's wonderful, isn't it?" a voice exclaimed, coming from behind me.

We turned to see two elderly women approach. One of the ladies, the one who had spoken, was wearing a dark maroon Aran sweater, with black pants. Her companion was similarly attired, wearing a royal blue Aran sweater with gray slacks. Jillian beamed a smile at the two women.

"Saoirse! Aine! I'm so glad you could make it!"

"We wouldn't miss it!" the woman in the blue sweater assured us. She looked straight at me and held out a hand. "Aine Bradigan. This is my sister, Saoirse."

I shook both of their hands and returned the smile. "Zack Anderson."

"I've heard your name, dear," Aine began. "We adore your wine!"

I gave the two ladies a slight bow. "Why thank you. I love your names, by the way. I've tried to learn Irish Gaelic, but it turned out to be more difficult than I had given it credit."

"If you ever want to learn," Saoirse began, "then you have but to ask. We were both teachers for over 40 years."

"How fascinating!" Jillian began. "I never knew."

"Pish posh," Aine chortled, as she waved dismissively at us with an arthritic hand. "There's much you don't know about us, dearie. Did you know Saoirse developed most of these recipes herself?"

Jillian nodded. "I did, yes."

"Did you cook all of this?" I asked, amazed.

Saoirse shook her head. "Some. I had help, dear boy. The ladies of my bridge club wanted to learn how to properly cook, so Aine and I held our first class since retiring."

I turned to Jillian. "Was that the class you took last month? The cooking class?"

"That's the one," Jillian confirmed. "I've been waiting for the best time to introduce some of my new dishes. Ms. Bradigan, I loved your class. You should consider offering more!"

"We'll see, dear. We'll see."

"How long have you been in the state?" I wanted to know.

"We retired almost ten years ago," Saoirse began. "I believe it has been nearly five years since we decided to move here. It was time for a change, wasn't it, Aine? Aine? Did you doze off again?"

"I did no such thing. Put your glasses on. Maybe then you'll be able to see something."

"I think it's wonderful you were able to retire together," Jillian said, drawing smiles from both sisters. "I only have one brother, and I don't think I'll ever be able to say we live in the same state again. He lives on the other side of the country."

"What grade did you teach?" I asked.

Both women stared at me with blank expressions. I ended up chuckling.

"My fault. European schools have a different way to classify the kids. Umm, what year did you teach?"

"We both taught at Buttleston," Saoirse proudly informed me. "Third years, if you must know. We had so many wonderful years, teaching generation after generation of children."

"Why'd you stop?" I asked.

"Oh, heavens," Aine exclaimed, "I couldn't take another year of those brats with their infernal devices."

I snorted with surprise and burst out laughing.

"Kids and their phones," Jillian observed. "They all seem to have them nowadays."

"It was time," Aine told us, as she added a forlorn sigh for effect. "Anyway, did I hear you talking about my colcannon? It was our mother's recipe. You'll find none finer in all of Ireland."

"You'll try it, won't you, Mr. Anderson?" Saoirse asked. "I spent several hours on that dish. I think it's my best yet!"

Stuck, I turned to Jillian, hopeful that she had a plan to get me out of having to eat a dish with cooked cabbage.

"Let me get you a fresh plate," my darling fiancée said, as she hurriedly returned to the stacks of paper plates and selected another. "Here, Zachary. Your hands are full. Would you like me to dish you some?"

Caught like a deer in headlights, I could only nod. "That would be ... lovely. Thank you so much."

Jillian batted her eyes at me and then waited for me to take a bite. Not one to back down from a challenge, especially when three pairs of female eyes were upon me, I sighed inwardly, scooped up some of the mashed potatoes on my fork, while trying to surreptitiously avoid the huge chunks of cabbage. Before I could change my mind, I popped it in my mouth. Thankfully, I also noticed Jillian had procured a fresh bottle of water when she had grabbed my new plate and had already opened it.

"What do you think?" Saoirse anxiously asked. "You're speechless, I can tell. I cannot begin to tell you how many people have tried that dish. It's been a family favorite for years!"

"Decades!" Aine added.

The two elderly sisters moved off. The moment they were out of earshot, I held out a hand. Jillian immediately slapped the water bottle down, as though I was a doctor and had just asked for a scalpel. Guzzling half the bottle, I checked to make sure the coast was clear before letting out an exclamation of disgust.

"What do you think?" Jillian quietly asked.

I gave the colcannon a look of derision before glancing up at Jillian. "It was just as I expected it to be. I just don't understand how anyone could eat cooked cabbage. Why would the Irish people subject themselves to such horrors?"

"Probably because, during the Great Potato Famine, they had little to eat. When you're starving, you'll eat just about anything to survive."

That sobered me. I, of all people, should've known that. After all, I had just written a book about a single, resourceful woman living in Ireland during the famine. This particular book required lots of research, and in doing so, I learned all about the Irish and their affinity for potatoes. In fact, Vance was due to present the first copy of the book to Tori, whom I based the protagonist after, on his and Tori's fifteenth anniversary, which would fall on June 25th this summer.

"Yeah, I can get on board with that. Hey, I promised Harry I'd bring some food over after we leave. What do you think he'd like?"

"Harrison will eat anything," Jillian said, after a few moments had passed. "And right now, since the twins are three months old, they could use all the help they can get."

"And they're getting it," I reminded my companion, with a smile. "I'm always running errands for them, or doing minor repairs."

"Tori and I are always cooking something for them, too," Jillian added.

"Vance gives a hand whenever I can't. Between all of us, I'd say they're doing pretty good."

"It's wonderful that our friends have such a strong support system," Jillian decided.

"Oh, they're getting a bill," I declared, but not before plastering a goofy grin on my face.

"How did Monday night go?"

Earlier this week, I volunteered to help Harry

and Julie's older kids with their homework. Hardy, their oldest child, was currently in high school and had to write a paper on the Bermuda Triangle. Having absolutely no free time whatsoever, who did Harry end up calling? Who else but the published writer. As for Drew, Harry's eight-year-old daughter, she had a math test she needed help with. So, in between giving pointers to Hardy, and the importance of properly citing your source of information, I tutored Drew with her math.

Talk about doing your good deeds for the day.

Back to the present. Deciding our friends might like some of the authentic Irish cuisine instead of having to cook, Jillian and I each set off to fill a plate with food. Surprising even myself, I only picked out items I thought Harry might like, while steering clear of the black pudding, tripe, and anything else that turned my stomach. What can I say? I'm a good friend.

I kissed Jillian goodbye and, properly armed with plates of food, headed for Harry and Julie's house first. Once I had passed the plates over to one harassed-looking father of twins, I was off again, only this time, my Jeep was headed to Vance and Tori's house.

Pulling up to my detective friend's house on Pinetop Way, I saw that Vance's two daughters were playing in the front yard, with the corgis. The Samuelson family dog, Anubis, a large German Shepherd, was currently sprawled out on the ground while both corgis ran circles around his prone form. Laughing hysterically, Tiffany and Victoria, ages eleven and thirteen respectively, were timing their jumps *across* Anubis' body, while trying to avoid contact with the corgis. Also of note was the simple fact that Anubis was lying at the base of an enormous leaf pile, no doubt the result of what the girls had originally been doing in the front yard.

Sherlock, however, saw what they were trying to do and adjusted his speed accordingly. Just like that, Sherlock's snout nudged Victoria's ankle, and down she went, only she had made the mistake of running toward the leaf pile, with the intent to circumnavigate it. Thanks to Sherlock's little push, Victoria tripped and, for all intents and purposes, became swallowed up by the leaf pile. Victoria's little sister, Tiffany, shrieked with glee, which attracted the attention of both corgis, and they promptly took off after her. The slender girl zig-zagged her way across the yard, with both Sherlock and Watson in hot pursuit. As they neared Anubis, the large German Shepherd took it upon himself to lend a paw to his two packmates.

Just as Tiffany braced herself to jump over their family's dog, Anubis leapt to his feet. In case you were wondering whether or not Anubis was hurt in the impending collision, I should remind you that German Shepherds were a part of the herding group. Those dogs are built like bricks, and were bred to withstand a blow by those animals which they were supposed to be herding.

I could hear the solid *thump* the impact made all the way from the driveway.

In this case, Anubis shook himself off, straddled the girl's still figure, and offered her an apology. Moments later, both corgis joined in on the fun. The squeals the girl was making alerted their mother, Tori, who appeared in the doorway just as I stepped out of my Jeep. Watson noticed my presence first, and hustled over to give me a greeting. It was also when I noticed the leaf pile began to move on its own. All three dogs momentarily paused as they watched Victoria emerge, spitting leaves. Disinterested, the dogs returned to *attacking* the younger sister.

"Hey there, Tiffany," I said, by way of a greeting. I helped the girl to her feet. "Don't ever say dogs don't talk to each other. I swear Anubis was helping Sherlock and Watson slow you down."

"He jumped up at a bad time," Tiffany observed, with a grin. "Do you have to take Sherlock and Watson home now?"

I nodded. "It's getting late, and I'm sure they're both 'h'."

"H?" Victoria repeated, as she appeared next to her sister. She continued to brush bits of leaves off her clothes as she looked inquisitively up at me. "What is that supposed to mean?"

Remembering that the older daughter was learning Spanish, I grinned. "*Hambre.*"

"What did he say?" Tiffany asked her sister.

Victoria's eyes widened. She looked down at the corgis and gave them each a scratching.

"They want their d-i-n-n-e-r."

Tiffany nodded. "Oh. You mean they're hungry."

All three dogs perked up.

"And that's why he was trying to *not* say the word, Tiff," Tori laughed.

"Were they any trouble?" I asked, as I clipped leashes on my two dogs.

"Not at all. Any time you'd like to drop them off for some play time, you don't even need to ask. Feel free."

An elderly couple appeared on the sidewalk, walking silently, hand-in-hand. The man had his head down, and was walking with the use of a cane. At their current pace, and from the direction they were walking, the two of them would be coming within range of the corgis in just a matter of moments.

"Aren't you two the cutest things?" the woman said, as she smiled. She used her long fingers to stroke the fur on Watson's neck. "Walter? Don't you think so?"

"Of course," the man said, sounding like he believed the exact opposite.

What was the saying? If my dog doesn't trust you, then I most certainly wouldn't? It was something like that. Well, in this case, if this elderly gentleman wanted to be stand-offish, then so be it. He could do it elsewhere. Quietly, and without being noticed, I slipped my phone from my pocket and took a few pictures.

"You have yourselves a wonderful day," the woman abruptly said, as she and her husband strode away.

I nodded in their direction. "Thanks. I will. See you, Tori. Tiffany? Victoria? *Hasta luego!*"

"I thought you didn't know any Spanish," Tori said, surprised.

"And that constitutes the entirety of my vocabulary," I admitted. "I'm learning. Jillian bought me a program for my tablet, which is teaching me the language. Philosopher's Rock. It's quite amazing."

"I'll look into it. See you later, Zack!"

Twenty minutes later found me pulling into my driveway. Parking my Jeep inside the garage, I was about ready to unclip the corgis' leashes when, for some inexplicable reason, the dogs perked up. Sherlock then let out a warning woof. Was someone here?

A quick check of the garage's interior confirmed that it was just the three of us. I opened the driver's door to my Ruxton and checked inside, curious to see if I had left something in it. Nope. About to admit defeat, I heard Sherlock fire off another warning woof. Something had spooked Sherlock, and that, unfortunately, had spooked me.

"All right, guys. Something's up. Let's go look around, all right? Maybe Caden forgot to receive a delivery for the winery. Why else would you ..."

I trailed off after both dogs physically pulled me over to my front door. There, on the welcome mat, of all things, was a medium-sized crate. Walking the dogs over to the object, I let them both sniff around the container to see if there were any other reactions.

There weren't, aside from neither dog breaking eye-contact with the thing, as if they thought there was another dog inside. That thought did make me stop and consider. Was there something I needed to be wary of?

Retracing my steps to the garage, I grabbed the first tool I could find, which was a rake with a wooden handle. Holding the landscaper's tool by the metal head, I used the long handle to jab the wooden box a few times. When nothing happened, I knelt next to the crate and held my ear to it. Seeing how I couldn't hear the telltale *tick-tock* of an explosive device (I really *did* watch too many movies), I decided it was safe to bring it inside the house. After all, there *was* a shipping label on the thing. I just couldn't make out the writing: too mangled.

Once inside, the dogs crowded around me as I carefully set the crate on the floor in my living room and set to work opening it up. This particular crate had its lid secured with screws, so once those had been removed, the top could be lifted off. Reaching inside, I lifted out a silver, cigar-sized box adorned with all manner of shapes, symbols, markings, and what looked like a few runes. Of note, on the largest side of the chest, which could be considered the front, was a very recognizable symbol: a shamrock.

One problem became immediately apparent: there was no lid. How was I supposed to get the blasted thing open?

"Well, well. What have we here, guys?"

# TWO

W hat do you think? Should I be worried? I mean, this crazy thing showed up on my doorstep last night. I can't find a way to open it, so I thought I'd bring it here."

Vance was silent as he studied the silver box I had placed on his desk. After a few moments, he gently rotated it this way and that, all the while pushing and prodding the various adornments that seemed to be covering every square inch of surface. Catching sight of the large shamrock on the front of the chest, the rotating stopped.

"It's a shamrock."

"Thanks, Captain Obvious," I scoffed. "Can you tell me anything else about it?"

My detective friend leaned close and stared at the intricately carved Celtic symbol. "Is this silver?"

"I think the whole thing is silver. That's gotta mean it's worth something, right?"

"I can't imagine there are that many silver boxes that look like this. Have you tried looking it up online?"

"I spent half the night trying to do just that," I confessed.

"And?" Vance prompted.

"Couldn't find a thing."

"Who sent it to you?"

I reached into a pocket and pulled out a ripped, folded piece of paper.

"I was able to peel this off the crate it was shipped in. I can't make much out of it."

"There's no shipping company listed?"

I tapped the top left corner. "It's been smudged. I have no idea what it says, other than the company name is two words."

Vance held out a hand. "May I?"

I handed him the shipping invoice and leaned back in my chair as Vance studied the packing slip. After a few moments, Vance picked up his desk phone and pressed a button. We waited, in silence, for whomever he called to answer the phone.

"Brigette? Could you come in here, please?"

The cradle was replaced. Curious, I stared at my friend and crossed my arms over my chest.

"Did you find something?"

Vance suddenly grinned at me and offered a shrug. "Maybe. We'll see."

A young woman in her early twenties appeared

at the door.

"Detective? You called?"

"Yes, thanks. Zack, not a word. Brigette? Your eyes are much better than mine. Can you make out what it says right here?"

I snorted with laughter, which earned me a beaming smile from the girl, and a glower from Vance.

"Printed in Chesterfield," Brigette read, as she looked at the paper.

Vance sat up straight. "What? Where does it say that?"

Brigette tapped the bottom right corner of the paper. "Here, next to the shipping date."

"It has a shipping date?" Vance asked, incredulous. "I didn't see that, either."

"Where do you see that?" I asked, as I hurriedly stood. "I must've stared at that paper for the better part of two hours last night."

Brigette handed me the slip. "It's right here. February 3rd. It *is* rather small."

"Small? All I see is a thin, black line. Looks like a signature line."

"That's what I thought it was," Vance admitted, as he leaned over my shoulder to see for himself where the date was allegedly printed.

I turned to look up at my friend and gave him a grin. "So, is it safe to assume your eyes are just as lousy as mine?"

Vance looked at the paper, back at Brigette, then back at the paper. "Obviously. And no, I won't tell Jillian if you won't tell Tori."

"I find those terms acceptable," I decided, with a chuckle.

"Is there anything else that's useful on there?" Vance wanted to know, as he looked back at the young woman. "We're trying to find out who might have shipped this box to Zack."

Brigette took the seat next to mine and studied the paper. "Well, I can make out a circular stamp right here. It's faint, and hard to see, but it's there."

Both Vance and I leaned over the desk, at precisely the same time. What was the result? You guessed it. We knocked heads.

"Ow!"

"Ouch!"

"You two are funny," Brigette decided. "Perhaps one at a time?"

I rubbed my forehead. "You're up, pal. You first."

Vance scrutinized the paper for close to a minute before giving up.

"If it's there, I can't see it."

"Let me try," I said, as I held out a hand. "Chances are, I'm going to have just as much luck as you in trying to see this mark."

"Stamp," Brigette corrected.

"Whatever. Nuh-uh, I don't see it, either. What, is it invisible ink and you just happen to be able to see it without a UV light?"

Brigette giggled. "I've always had really good eyesight. I can't help it."

Vance pushed a notebook and a pencil over to the girl.

"Could you draw what you see? So those of us who are visually-impaired can see what you're looking at?"

"Sure. Let's see. It says *this* along the top. There's a curve coming down, like this. Then, this word is here. And finally, there are some letters along the bottom curve. There you go. What do you think?"

Vance took one look at the sketch Brigette had made and whistled. "I have no idea how to pronounce that, let alone know what it is."

"Spell it," I suggested.

"All right. Uh, C-w-m-b-r-a-n. Any ideas what it could be?"

I pulled my phone out and searched for the word online. "It's a town in Wales." I looked up. "Wales? This is Welsh?"

Vance tapped the top of the diagram, where Brigette had written International Delivery. "There you have it. Your box is from Wales. Thanks for your help, Brigette."

"My pleasure, Detective."

"What now?" Vance inquired, after the girl had departed. "Have you shown Jillian yet?"

"That's next," I admitted. "She's one wickedly smart woman. Perhaps she will recognize it?"

Vance shrugged. "It's worth a shot. Keep me posted, pal."

"You got it."

Ten minutes later, I was parking the Jeep in front of Jillian's store. Gathering the dog's leashes tightly in my hand, the three of us, with me holding the wooden crate under my arm, stepped inside Jillian's specialty kitchen store. A girl wearing a purple apron approached, having heard the entry chime the door made after it opened. She caught sight of me, waved, and was about to turn on her heel when she noticed the dogs.

"Sherlock and Watson! Oh, it's good to see you two!"

The dogs were writhing with excitement.

"Can I watch them for you, Mr. Anderson?"

I gave Jillian's day manager, Cassie, a smile, dropped the leashes, and waited for the dogs to appear by her side. Knowing the dogs were in good hands, I started to look for Jillian. Cassie cleared her throat and pointed upstairs.

"Zachary!" Jillian exclaimed, as she rose from the table she was sitting at in her store's tiny café. "What a pleasant surprise! I'm glad you stopped by. What do you have there?"

"Something I want you to look at," I told her, as I set the wooden crate down on a nearby table. I reached inside and gingerly lifted the silver box free of its crate. "What do you make of this?"

"Oooo, it's pretty. Where did it come from?"

"It was waiting for me when I made it home last night."

"Someone sent this to you? Do you know who?"

"Someone from Wales," I answered, as I pulled

out a chair and sat down. "That's all I know."

"Do you have friends in Wales? I didn't know that."

"I don't," I clarified. "At least, I don't think I do. So, tell me. Does that thing look familiar to you?"

"No, it doesn't," Jillian said, after spending a few moments looking over the chest. "I know someone who you ought to ask."

"Who?" I wanted to know.

"Burt. Burt Johnson? Do you think we can ask him?"

"I don't see why not. He's a nice enough guy, if a touch intimidating. Do you think he'd know what this is?"

"It couldn't hurt to ask him. Hold on. I'll give him a call, just as soon as I find his number. Now, do I have it listed under his name or the name of his business? Ah, here it is. Hidden Relic Antiques. There's the number. Let's hope he ... Hello, Burt? It's Jillian Cooper. Are you available? Zachary is here, and he has something here I'd like you to take a look at. Neither of us know what it is, and we're hoping you might. Yes, that's right. You will? Thank you. I owe you a favor."

"You mean, *I* owe him a favor," I slyly corrected, as my fiancée terminated the call.

"It doesn't matter. I ... is this silver?"

"It sure looks like it, doesn't it? And look at this. There are pieces that move on the box. I noticed that last night. This round dial-looking thing rotates, and this square can be pushed in, like a button. The more I look, the more I notice. I just wish I knew what it all meant."

Several minutes later, we heard the entrance chime announce the arrival of another person. Jillian pushed away from the table and looked down the stairs.

"Burt? Is that you?"

"It's me, Ms. Cooper," a deep voice rumbled.

"We're up here."

Moments later, PV's largest, most daunting citizen was standing before us. Standing at six and a half feet tall, and weighing in around 350 pounds, Burt Johnson had to be the biggest, most muscular person I have ever clapped eyes on. I've never known how old he is, but if I had to guess, then I'd say late fifties, or early sixties. He wore his short, gray hair in a military-style buzz cut, had huge sideburns on either side of his face, and had a variety of tattoos on his arms, making him appear as though he would be more suited on a motor-cycle.

I know what you're thinking. I really shouldn't be this judgmental, and what's more, I would be the first to admit it. In fact, I have actually apologized to Burt, himself, for having a preconceived notion what he must be like. Thankfully, Burt took my comments in stride and laughed off my concerns.

Pomme Valley's expert in antiques strode over to our table, but before anyone could say anything, we saw his eyes latch onto the silver box.

Without asking permission, he slowly sank down onto one of the table's chairs and started to reach for it. A split second later, he hesitated and looked over at me. I nodded permission, to which he nodded once in return, and slid the box over to him.

"Where did you get this?" Burt asked, clearly awed.

"Based on the shipping invoice, someone in Wales sent this to me."

"Makes sense," Bart said, as he nodded. "After all, this is British. Do you see this shamrock? It's obviously Irish. And this cross, on the back? English. There's also a thistle back here, which is ..."

The huge man trailed off and gave Jillian a sidelong glance, who smiled and nodded.

"Scottish."

"Correct. Three various themes, and all point to Great Britain."

"What about this?" I asked, as I leaned forward and twisted the circle encompassing the cross. Burt's eyes lifted with surprise as he noticed the ring of metal shift a quarter of an inch clockwise. "And there's also this." I then pressed a square of metal to the right of the thistle. It clicked loudly as it recessed into the surface.

Anxious to see if there were other movable parts, Burt began to gently poke and prod at the chest.

"This lion that I didn't notice before? Its tail is movable, like a lever. Can either of you tell if anything happens when I do this?"

Jillian and I stared intently at the chest while Burt maneuvered the tiny tail up and down.

"I don't see anything," I reported. "Then again, I don't know what I was expecting to happen."

Burt looked at Jillian. "Ms. Cooper? How about you?"

"I'm afraid I don't see anything, either."

"What does it mean?" I wondered aloud.

"The craftmanship is unbelievable," Burt was saying, his voice so soft that he was practically whispering. "There has to be a reason why the lion's tail moves, or the circle spins, or a shamrock leaf rotates the way it does."

"The shamrock rotates?" I repeated. "Did I hear that right?"

In response, Burt turned the chest around so that Jillian and I could see the Celtic shamrock on the front. Using two fingers, he gently gripped the right-most leaf and twisted. Sure enough, the leaf rotated just enough to make it stand apart from the other two. On a Celtic knot shamrock, it became quite obvious the leaf had been moved, seeing how the entire design was comprised of a single line weaving in and around itself, as most Celtic knots happened to be.

"Himitsu-Bako," Jillian announced.

Burt nodded, as his face lit up. "Precisely!"

"What's that?" I asked, when no further explanations were forthcoming.

"Himitsu-Bako," Jillian repeated. "Japanese personal secret boxes."

"And those are …?" I gently inquired.

"I'm sure you've seen them before," Burt began. "They range in size, but most are small, about the size of this chest. Each surface of the wooden box is finished with seamless wooden texture. Some have geometric designs, and others are plain."

"Exactly," Jillian confirmed. "They look like ordinary boxes, but they don't have lids. The only way to open a Himitsu-Bako box is to solve the puzzle."

"How is a simple box also a puzzle?" I wanted to know.

"Because certain parts move," Burt explained. "A narrow strip here, or a side panel there."

"They call them *steps*," Jillian added. "Each box has its own number of steps to solve."

"The most complex Himitsu-Bako I've ever solved had twenty-one steps," Burt said.

Jillian nodded. "Thirty-five for me."

"Makes me think I need to try one of these puzzle boxes," I mused.

"I still have mine at home," Jillian announced. "I'll let you borrow it so you can see what I mean."

I pointed at the chest. "So, you think the same principle used for these whatchamacallits are at play here?"

Burt and Jillian both regarded me with a piteous expression.

"What? It's a legitimate question."

"If you're referring to the internal mechanics of Himitsu-Bako," Burt began, as if he was standing behind a podium with an audience of students, "and are applying them here, to this chest, then yes, I think that's a possibility."

I looked at Jillian and held up my hands. "Meaning what?"

"We think it might be a puzzle box."

"Oh. Why didn't you just say so?"

Burt grinned at me. "We did. Listen, if you ever want to sell this, Mr. Anderson, then I do hope you'll come to me. I would love to take this off your hands."

I tapped the chest. "If there's something in here worth hiding, and we manage to get it out, then sure, I'll be willing to entertain the notion."

Satisfied, Burt nodded. "That reminds me. About your Ruxton..."

"Hey, didn't I apologize for bumping your sign?" I protested. "I thought we were past that."

"Which time?" Jillian teased.

Burt's eyebrows shot up. I immediately held up my hands in a time-out gesture.

"Now, wait a minute. I only hit it the one time, and I did apologize for that. Besides, you straightened the sign yourself, didn't you?"

"Take a breath, Mr. Anderson," Burt soothed. "I don't care about the sign. I'm more concerned about your car."

"Oh. It's fine. I ended up taking it back to Rupert's Gas & Auto, and they were able to get it all fixed up for me. Took out the dents, replaced the starter, and gave the transmission a clean bill of health."

"Are you interested in selling it?" Burt politely inquired.

"Oh. You want to buy the Ruxton? Thanks, but I'll have to decline. Jillian gave me that car, and I have every intention of keeping it. But, I'll tell you what. If, like the chest, I ever decide to sell it, then you'll be the first person I call."

Mollified, Burt nodded. "I understand. Ms. Cooper? Mr. Anderson? I take my leave of you."

He stood, shook my hand, smiled at Jillian, and headed down the stairs, presumably back to his store. I had to flex my right hand for a few minutes in order to restore circulation. Man alive, that dude is strong. It felt as if all my fingers had fused together.

"So, the chest is British," Jillian began, "and was shipped to you from Wales. How does that help us?"

I shrugged. "I don't think it does. The only helpful thing we learned here is that we're pretty sure it's a puzzle box. I, for one, would love to know what it's hiding."

Jillian suddenly snapped her fingers and her million dollar smile was back.

"I have an idea. If you really want to know what's inside, perhaps you could get it x-rayed?"

"And how am I supposed to do that?" I inquired. "It's not like we all have x-ray machines in our homes."

"No, but airports do. Medford County Airport

is less than twenty minutes away. They have an x-ray machine, which they use to check luggage. Perhaps you could get the box examined there?"

Suddenly, I was grinning like a schoolboy. What a wonderful idea! Why didn't I think of that?

I glanced at the large, analog clock on the wall next to the menu board in Jillian's café. It wasn't even lunchtime yet. I had time!

"Thanks. That's a terrific idea. I think the dogs and I will go for a drive."

"Let me know what you find out," Jillian called, as I trooped down the stairs.

I found the corgis draped across Cassie's lap in one of the recliners in the plush reading area at the back of Cookbook Nook. Sherlock's head lifted as I approached. He watched me for a few moments before reluctantly rousing himself enough to jump down to the floor. Watson followed several moments later.

"The next time you need someone to puppysit," the high-schooler began, "please give me a call. I love your two dogs!"

"You're on," I promised, as I took the leashes. "Sherlock? Watson? Let's go."

As we headed east on Main Street, on the route I usually take when driving to the neighboring city of Medford, the dogs started woofing. Surprised, I ended up almost getting into an accident as I rapidly checked mirrors, checked my blind spots as I was driving, and checked the surrounding area for strange happenings. So, what had caught their attention? I was about to say that I didn't know, when I made a left turn off of Main Street and noticed I was being followed. The car doing the following was a late model black Mercedes-Benz sedan, with heavily tinted windows. Seriously, they might as well have been driving a windowless panel van. Nothing screams suspicion like those two examples of vehicles.

"Who do you think they are?" I quietly asked the dogs, as though I was afraid we'd be overheard.

Sherlock propped himself up on his squat hind legs and looked over the Jeep's backseat at the cars behind us. After a few seconds of indecision, Watson joined him. Now, more than ever, I had to be careful of my driving. One simple tap on the brakes, and the dogs would go *flying*.

"Guys? I don't supposed you'd like to get down from there, would you? If someone cuts me off, then you two are gonna be in for a rough ride." I was ignored. "Are you sure that black car is following us? What do you say we find out?"

I hit the signal and made another left, which had me now heading south once more, which was back the way we had come. Approaching Main Street once more, we made a right and, for all intents and purposes, it would appear to any outside observer that we were headed back to Jillian's store. I gave it another few moments when I noticed the traffic light in front of me start to change colors. I stomped on the gas and waited to see what the sedan would do.

Sure enough, the dark automobile jetted through the intersection just as the light turned red. It came to a stop several cars behind me and, together, we waited for the next light to turn green. As we drove by Jillian's telltale purple building, home of her store and a few others, I decided that it was time to introduce my detective friend to my new admirers. I tapped a few buttons on my stereo and waited for the call to connect.

"Zack? Hey, buddy, what's up?"

"Vance, I think I have someone tailing me."

"What? Are you sure? It couldn't be someone just heading in the same direction as you?"

"I was on my way out of town when the dogs spotted them," I said, while I drummed my fingers on the steering wheel as I waited for the traffic light to change. "I made a few other turns, and then sped through an intersection just as it was changing, and wouldn't you know it, the Mercedes followed us."

"A Mercedes, huh?"

"Black, with tinted windows."

"Where are you at now?"

"We just passed Cookbook Nook. We made a right on 3rd, and are currently heading north.

"Meaning, you're going to hit D Street and, let me guess, you'll turn right so you can pass the police station, right?"

"Right," I confirmed. "Care to help me out, pal? Is there something I can do to get these people off our backs?"

"I was getting a cup of coffee, which means I'm by the front door right now. I'm heading outside to see this for myself."

"Perfect. We'll be there in about two minutes."

"Got it. What do you think your new pal wants?"

"What do you think?" I returned, exasperated. "They want the chest, what else? I haven't had anything else mysteriously appear in my life. It *has* to be what those people want. I think I'm going to need to find a place to stash it."

"I hear you. Hey, I see your Jeep coming up 3rd. Okay, just tell me how far back the Mercedes is, all right?"

"No problem. They're … what? What are they doing? Vance, I don't get it. They just turned on C Street, as though they knew exactly where I was going!"

"Hmm. How sure are you that they were following you?"

"A hundred percent. Why do you ask?"

"Pull over. I think I know why they pulled away at the last minute."

Once parked on the side of the road, the dogs and I watched Vance hurry over to my Jeep. He motioned for us to stay inside while he slowly walked around my vehicle. What was he doing? Was he looking for something?

Vance appeared at my driver side door and then made the hand motion to roll down the window.

"What …?" I began, but before I could finish,

Vance held up a finger to his lips.

My detective friend hurried around the car and carefully opened the second passenger door so that he could see the dogs, who naturally went ballistic once they saw him. Still saying nothing, Vance gently picked up Sherlock and moved him to the front passenger seat. Watching silently, I noticed Sherlock's ears jump straight up. Within moments, he was staring at my air freshener, currently dangling from the rearview mirror.

Pulling the vanilla-scented air freshener free of the mirror, Vance held it up close to his face as he gently rotated it this way and that. Grunting softly, I saw him picking at something, as though a drop of glue had fastened itself to the surface, and he was trying to scrape it off.

Something akin to a short, fat, green needle was extricated from within the freshener. I could see a tiny, blinking red light and just like that, I knew what Vance was doing. He had suspected my Jeep had been bugged. No wonder the Mercedes had sped off. They had been listening when I called Vance! My detective friend held a finger to his lips when he noticed I was about to ask a question. He studied the thin bug for a moment or two before he snapped it in half, as if it was a pencil. The red dot blinked twice and then went dark.

"How long has this been there?" Vance curiously asked.

"I didn't know I had it." I hooked a thumb at the corgis. "Neither did they. How did you know Sherlock would find it?"

"Dog Wonder? Are you kidding me? That corgi is the smartest dog I have ever encountered, and don't ever tell Tori I said that. She thinks the world of Anubis, but between you and me, our dog is Lennie, while yours is George."

"*Of Mice and Men*," I said. "I get the analogy, only I don't think it's true."

Vance waggled the high-tech bug in front of my face.

"If you'd like, I'll take this off your hands. Maybe our tech boys can figure out where it came from."

"It's all yours, pal. Thanks for the backup."

Vance held out a fist, which I quickly bumped. He then looked at the dogs and immediately produced two biscuits. For the first time ever, Sherlock ignored the biscuit and, instead, looked over at the closest parking lot, which was where the employees of the police station stored their vehicles.

"You don't want the biscuit?" Vance incredulously asked. "Dude, get him over to see Harry, pronto!"

I chuckled, but then noticed that Sherlock seemingly wanted out. Watson, intent on accompanying her packmate, was right there, with him. Turning off the ignition and exiting the Jeep, I set both dogs on the ground and was immediately pulled toward the rows of parked cars.

"What are you doing?" Vance wanted to know,

as he fell into step behind us.

I pointed at the dogs. "Go ahead and ask them. If they indicate what's on their minds, then please have them inform me, all right?"

Vance laughed, but then sobered as we were pulled over to a very familiar beige Oldsmobile.

"Why are we at my car?" my friend wondered aloud. "What's ..."

Vance trailed off as Sherlock thrust his nose under the front driver-side wheel well and woofed. Frowning, Vance squatted next to his car's front tire and, using the LED from his phone, inspected his car's wheel-well. I watched my friend give a visible start, and then mutter a curse. Reaching in, Vance retrieved a small black square. It had a tiny antenna and blinking green light. He glared angrily at me before he inspected *his* bug for a moment or two. Pulling out his pocket knife, he pried the cover off the black cube and made a flicking motion with the blade. I noticed something small and silver go tumbling, end over end, until it hit the ground and rolled away. By the time I looked back at the second bug, I noticed the blinking green light was gone.

"Your car was bugged, too," I guessed.

"I was gonna break it, like I did yours, but decided to see if our lab boys can get anything off of it," Vance explained. "Who the heck are these people, Zack?"

I gave my friend a helpless shrug.

"Follow me, pal. I'm gonna pull my car around

to the back. We're gonna let the crime scene boys check them to see if we've picked up any more unwanted friends."

# THREE

So, I thought we already did this," I began, as I fished a long, orange extension cable between several rows of white folding tables.

"Last Wednesday?" Jillian asked. "That was a trial run; a rehearsal. I was making sure Cookbook Nook could handle a gathering of that magnitude."

"Proof of concept," I said, nodding.

"Exactly."

"And so all these people cooked their dishes again?" I asked.

Jillian pointed at a nearby table, where an even larger bowl of colcannon was sitting.

"Does that look familiar?"

I immediately checked the surroundings. "Oh, tell me the Bradigan sisters aren't nearby. I just know they'll try to make me eat that stuff again."

"Is it really that bad?" Jillian asked. Her lovely face was smiling and I could see she was trying so hard to suppress the giggle that was trying so hard to escape.

"It is if you don't like cabbage," I returned.

"Then, you'd better hide," Jillian told me. "Here they come."

I dropped straight down to the ground, as though Wile E. Coyote himself had placed a one-ton anvil in my hands.

"Stay there for a moment," Jillian quietly instructed. "Saoirse! Aine! I'm so glad you made it back!"

"We wouldn't dream of missing your céilí," Aine assured us.

"I think I can speak for my sister," Saoirse began, "when I say we both enjoy being useful again. Thank you for allowing us to help."

"Are you kidding?" Jillian exclaimed. "You two are our guests of honor! Having so much experience in Ireland makes you two my secret weapons!"

"Put us to work, dear," Aine instructed.

"I don't see your handsome fiancé anywhere," Saoirse observed. "Will he be able to make it tonight?"

"I'm sure Zachary will find time to stop by," Jillian assured the two elderly sisters.

"See that he does," Aine said. "Now, what can we do?"

Jillian pointed at the rows of tables that had

been set up all throughout her store.

"You two are officially in charge of ensuring all dishes brought to the céilí are properly heated. The catering company has provided boxes and boxes of warming plates. If you need a buffet warmer, they are over there, in that stack."

"Do you have any tablecloths?" Saoirse asked.

"Tablecloths? You ask if I have tablecloths? Please. They're on the table behind you, arranged by type, texture, and color."

"We're on it," Aine announced. "You don't have to worry about a thing, dear."

After the sisters had moved off, Jillian lightly rapped her knuckles on the table I had been hiding under.

"The coast is clear. I'd keep a low profile, if I were you."

"You have my eternal thanks."

"If you'd like to relieve Rose, that'd be fine. Tell her I need her to keep an eye on International. I've already had half a dozen people ask me which Irish cookbooks we keep in stock."

"Gotcha."

"Oh, Zachary! Here comes a couple I'd like you to meet! Tell you what. Head over to the recliners and I'll bring them over to meet you."

"They're not going to guilt me into eating anything, are they?"

"The food is foreign," Jillian began, "but I guarantee you'll like it. Maggie has got to be the best cook I know. The icing on the cake is that, like the

Bradigans, she and her husband have lived in Ireland for most of their lives."

Looking past the boxes, and the tables, and the overall clutter of a party that was still being readied, I noticed an elderly man holding the door open for his wife. It made me smile. I don't know what it was about that particular chivalrous act, but it made me automatically like this particular couple. In fact, the two octogenarians held hands as soon as they entered Cookbook Nook and, catching sight of Jillian, veered in her direction.

"Mr. and Mrs. O'Sullivan!" I heard Jillian exclaim. "I'm so pleased you could make it!"

"Never turned down an invite to a céilí yet," Mr. O'Sullivan announced, with a very noticeable Irish lilt to his voice. "I have no intention of starting now."

I hurried over to Jillian's duly-designated reading section, which had four oversized plush armchairs circling a large, antique coffee table. Once there, I could see that my two corgis were once again schmoozing with Jillian's employees. This time, they were cuddling with someone I hadn't met yet.

"Oh, they've trained you well," I began, as I approached the dogs.

Sherlock and Watson perked up. The girl, a flaming redhead wearing thin black-framed eyeglasses, looked up at me and smiled.

"You must be Mr. Anderson. You're the lucky man who gets to go home with these two adorable fluff-muffins?"

"Adorable fluff-muffins," I repeated, with a chuckle. "That's cute. I'm sure those two just ate that up." After a few moments, I held out my hand. "Zachary Anderson."

"Rose Murphy. The pleasure is mine, Mr. Anderson. Or, should I say, Ms. Wadsworth?"

"Not you, too," I groaned, but not before I gave the girl a smile. "Let me guess. Jillian told you."

"She's proud of you," Rose stated, as she rose from her recliner and tried to remove the dog hair that had collected on her clothes. "She talks about you all the time. I told her my favorite genre of books is romance, and that's when she let it slip that I had more than likely read something of yours."

"And have you?"

Rose nodded. "The vast majority of your titles, yes."

"How long have you worked for Jillian?"

"About three weeks now."

"Is she a good person to work for?" I asked.

Rose nodded. "Absolutely. She talks to me like she's my best friend, and I can tell she genuinely cares about me."

"That sounds like Jillian, no doubt about it. Well, thank you for watching the dogs for me."

"Anytime, Mr. Anderson!"

"Oh. Rose? Jillian told me to tell you that she needs you to keep an eye on 'international.' I assume you know what that means?"

Rose nodded. "Yes. The International Cookbook section has been gaining in popularity the past year. Now, with this Irish festival happening today, I wouldn't be surprised if we had a run on all things Irish. You can tell her I'm on my way."

Since I didn't see Jillian anywhere, I pulled out my phone and texted Rose's response. There was no reply, but that wasn't surprising, seeing how many people were streaming into the store and how easily Jillian could be pulled away from the counter. Not only that, there was a significant increase of noise.

Naturally, right after that, I heard a peal of laughter, and I knew Jillian was close. Remembering she wanted me to meet the elderly couple who had just arrived, I looked at my two dogs and gave them each a pat on the head. Sherlock and Watson had both curled up on either side of my recliner, content to enjoy one of their favorite pastimes: people-watching.

More and more people wandered by, and as each of them noticed the dogs, everyone, and I do mean *everyone*, stopped to offer them a greeting, followed by a thorough scratching behind the ears. Sitting where I was, on the recliner, I had a clear view of Cookbook Nook's front entrance. I should also mention the céilí wasn't slated to begin for another hour. This crowd must really be in the mood for a party!

Suddenly, Sherlock and Watson perked up. They were seemingly staring through a small group of people who were headed our way. Glancing down at the dogs, I could see both had risen to their feet and were studying the approaching individuals. That's when the small group veered left, deeper into the store, and the three people behind them came into view. Jillian was there, and she was escorting an elderly couple.

The old woman stepped forward first. She was standing before me and inspecting me as though she was a general and I was the infantry, getting ready to head out to battle an unknown enemy.

"And who might this be?" a surprisingly strong and clear female voice asked.

I motioned for the dogs to stay put and then stood up. Holding out a hand, I smiled at the woman.

"Zachary Anderson. Down there are Sherlock and Watson."

"The writer!" the eighty-something woman exclaimed, delighted. "And your two famous dogs! We've heard so much about Sherlock and Watson, haven't we, dear?"

The husband nodded. "That we have, love, that we have."

The woman took my hand. "Maggie O'Sullivan. This is my husband, Niall."

I shook hands with Maggie's husband and was surprised yet again when I discovered his grip rivaled my own. I could only hope that, when I became an octogenarian myself, I had half the strength this elderly gentleman possessed. Niall politely shook my hand and nodded his head.

"I have read all your books, young man," Maggie continued, "and can say I have enjoyed them all."

"As have I," Mr. O'Sullivan added, with a sly smile.

"You have?" I repeated, certain these two couldn't possibly know what type of books I write, very steamy romances.

Correctly guessing what I was thinking, Mr. O'Sullivan nodded. "Oh, yes, dear boy. Your books always ... and pardon me for using an automotive analogy, get my Maggie's engine running. Let's just say that I benefit greatly."

Holy crap on a cracker. Was Niall insinuating what I *think* he was insinuating? I felt my face flame up and I knew, without a doubt, my skin was as red as a lobster. It was definitely time to change the subject.

"So, Mr. O'Sullivan, Jillian tells me you and your wife are from Ireland. What part, if you don't mind me asking?"

"Not at all," Maggie said, as she smiled warmly at me. "We've traveled extensively throughout our fair country, but we decided to settle in Lifford, County Donegal."

"I'm not familiar with Lifford," I admitted. "Or County Donegal, for that matter. Is that south Ireland, or is it in the north?"

"North," Niall answered.

"Lifford is a small village," Maggie wistfully began, "located fifteen miles from Letterkenny.

Our population has never grown larger than two thousand individuals, and that suited us just fine."

"No one locked their doors," Niall recalled.

"There was no crime," Maggie added.

"Townsfolk helped each other," Niall continued. "If there was a job to be done, then there would always be plenty of hands to see it through."

"Sounds wonderful," I sighed.

"It's not like here," Maggie said, but then blushed. "I'm sorry. No offense was intended."

"It's okay, Mrs. O'Sullivan," Jillian assured the friendly senior. "None was taken."

Niall clasped my shoulder and gave it a friendly squeeze. "You've been to our fair country?"

"County Cork," I confirmed. "And Dublin. To be honest, I liked Cork much better."

"Dublin has become too industrious," Maggie informed me. "I think you'd enjoy a visit to Lifford. There's much to see."

"I'm putting it on my To Do list," I assured them. "When did you move to Pomme Valley?"

Niall looked at Maggie and gave her a tender smile. "Must be going on fifteen years now."

"Almost twenty," Maggie confirmed. "And, there was a time when the crime rate of this city rivaled that of Lifford."

"I hear we have *you* to thank for that," Niall added, as he gave me an unreadable look.

An uncomfortable silence fell over the four of us as I stared at the old man glaring back at me.

After a few moments, his face split into a grin and he began to laugh.

"Hoo boy, he was right! Did you see the look on poor Zachary's face, love? I thought he was going to faint dead away!"

Unsure how I should respond, I suddenly heard a second person laughing. And a third. Then, a familiar person appeared, holding a plate of food. He grinned at me and held up his phone, suggesting he had recorded the encounter.

"Vance, I should have known you had a hand in that," I grumbled, only I couldn't manage to hide the grin on my face. I looked at my new Irish friends and inclined my head in Vance's direction. "Don't believe a word he says."

Niall blinked with confusion. "Indeed? He said you are the most intelligent person he has ever known since he became a closet romance reader."

I noted, with incredible delight, the smirk had disappeared from Vance's face and, instead, had been replaced with a look of abject horror.

"I said no such thing!" my detective friend insisted.

It was my turn to hold up my phone.

"You heard it right, ladies and gents! Pomme Valley's own Detective Vance Samuelson is an ardent admirer of romance novels and has read every one I have ever published!"

"Am not! Did not!"

Jillian burst out laughing, which had both O'Sullivans also giggling. Vance glowered at me and, I could tell, came *thiiiiiiis* close to giving me the one-fingered salute. Since I had my phone out, and was recording him, he just shook his head, knocked fists with me when no one was looking, and moved off.

A lively Irish tune began. To my ear, it sounded like a recorder, or perhaps a whistle. I couldn't tell if it was being piped in through Jillian's overhead speakers, or if the musician was there on site. After a few moments, the whistle was accompanied by a fiddle. Then, some type of drum began beating.

Curious how the dogs would react to the music, I glanced down. If anything, both dogs appeared to be calm and relaxed. They settled to the floor on either side of my chair once more and, if I didn't know any better, I'd say Sherlock was moments away from falling asleep.

I think both of them would have taken a nap, right there in the store, only due to their popularity, they had a steady stream of admirers and visitors. People kept coming up to me and asking permission to meet them. Both corgis looked up at their line of admirers, and then turned to look at me, as if to say thanks. As one, they both rolled over.

"Dogs," I muttered.

The crowd loved it.

I watched the two Bradigan sisters walk by. They smiled and waved enthusiastically at me. One of them, Saoirse, I believe, held up a plate of food, to which I could see included an inordinate amount of the nasty colcannon she had made. Never in my life have I been so grateful to see two people pass me by and *not* stop. There was no way I could stomach another mouthful of that particular recipe.

That's when I noticed the dogs. Both Sherlock and Watson had perked up when the two elderly sisters appeared, and watched them like hawks. Did they think they were going to spill their food? Or offer them some type of morsel?

"Put that thought out of your little puppy brains," I told the corgis. "You're not eating anything in here, is that understood?"

Sherlock silently regarded me for a few moments before he returned his attention to the passing people. I swear that dog's expression said, *we'll see about that.* For the next half an hour, we entertained a steady stream of visitors, from people we knew, like Captain Nelson of the police department, and Spencer Woodson, from Toy Closet, to complete unknowns, like the young family who had just arrived. The mother and father looked young, in their twenties, and had four kids, ranging in age from a toddler just learning to walk to a wide-eyed eight-year-old girl. The parents looked tired, but happy. They saw the dogs and immediately pointed them out to their kids. The three older children shied away, much to their parents' chagrin, but it was the toddler who surprised them all. The young girl blinked her eyes at Sherlock a few times before taking several staggering steps in his direction.

Sherlock yipped once and immediately dropped into a playful crouch.

I watched the mother battle her indecision about coming to her baby's aid, but the father held her back and, together, they watched what their youngest child was about to do. Nearing Sherlock's still form, the toddler tripped over her own feet and fell forward. Before either parent could react, the baby ended up sprawled over Sherlock's head and neck. The tri-colored corgi, much to my amazement, remained mired in place as he patiently waited for the baby to regain her balance. However, the toddler must have decided reclining on the nice, furry pillow was better than trying to walk, because she slid into a sitting position.

Sherlock's head and neck were still wrapped in a death-grip by the toddler.

"Omigod, Shae," the father exclaimed, as he finally decided to rush forward, but due to the amount of fur visible in the toddler's clenched fists, the parent hesitated in pulling his daughter away.

"What's the matter?" the mother asked.

"She's got ahold of the fur in both hands. I don't know how we're gonna get her to let go."

Both parents looked up at me with apologetic looks on their faces.

"We are so sorry," the father began. "If I was your dog, I probably would have freaked out long ago."

"Sherlock knows she's young," I explained. "Hmm. I have an idea how to make her let go, without hurting her *or* Sherlock."

"How?" the mother inquired.

I pointed at the plate of food the oldest daughter was holding.

"Is that pumpkin pie?" I asked.

The parents and the girl holding the plate looked down at the pie. After a few moments, when nothing was said, the mother nudged her daughter.

"Abby? Is it pumpkin pie?"

Abby shook her head. "It tastes like it, and smells like it, but ... it's not pie."

The mother took Abby's spoon and tried a tiny piece.

"Mousse. It's pumpkin mousse."

"That'll do," I decided. "Take a little of the mousse and smear some of it on your baby's cheek."

The father looked at me as though I was a few sandwiches short of a picnic. I winked at him and then pointed at Watson, who turned to look at me at the same time. Comprehending what I wanted to do, the father nodded. He carefully took the plastic utensil from his wife and scooped a tiny bit off the plate. Turning to me, he grinned, and then squatted next to his youngest child. He dabbed a little of the mousse on his baby's cheek and took a few steps back.

I looked down at my female corgi and cleared my throat. "Watson? Would you do the honors?"

Leaning forward, I touched the child's cheek. Watson was on her feet in a flash. A split second later, Watson was using her soft tongue to extract every last bit of pumpkin from the child's face. Understandably, this got young Shae's attention.

The two chubby fists released Sherlock's fur. For the record, Sherlock remained unconcerned the entire time. In fact, even after his fur had been released, he remained motionless, next to my recliner, as if youngsters pulling his fur were a daily occurrence.

"I'm really sorry 'bout that," the young father began, as he held his baby girl in his arms. "Although, your dog doesn't seem to be bothered."

"You guys are fine. No harm done." After the family had wandered away, I gave the corgis a solid scratch behind each ear. "Good job, you two."

Sherlock and Watson perked up. I ruffled their fur and was about to settle back in my recliner when I noticed neither of the dogs were paying attention to me. They were now watching the Bradigan sisters, who had just wandered by again. Based on their empty plates, I could only assume they were on the hunt for more dishes to try. After they passed out of sight, both corgis settled down. Weird. For whatever reason, I decided to take a few pictures.

Our next visitor was Jillian, who handed me a bottle of Coke Zero without breaking stride. She blew me a kiss and disappeared into the milling throngs of people. I looked at my bottle of soda and grinned. Now, where had she been hiding this?

Man alive, I love that woman.

Vance, Tori, and their two girls appeared. Victoria and Tiffany went straight for the dogs while Vance and Tori took the seats next to mine. Tori leaned back in her chair and sighed contentedly.

"Oh, this feels nice. You have the right idea, Zack. I've been on my feet all day, and let's just say they aren't happy."

"Mr. Anderson?" I heard one of Vance's daughters say. "What are your dogs doing?"

Intrigued, I leaned forward to see for myself. Sherlock and Watson were on their feet, but both had eyes for Tori, as though she was holding a big, juicy steak. Before you start complaining, or taking my name in vain, let me clarify: I have *never* fed my dogs steak before. Maybe a steak-flavored treat every so often, but never the real thing. In this case, based on the way my dogs were staring at Vance's wife, you'd think she had a juicy T-bone stuffed inside her purse.

"What's with them?" Vance wanted to know.

I looked over at Tori, who had her eyes closed. I nudged Vance and hooked a thumb at Tori. My detective friend looked over at his wife and, moments later, his brow furrowed with concern.

"Tor? Are you okay?"

Tori's eyes opened. "Of course. Why do you ask?"

In response, Vance pointed at the two dogs.

"It looks like they think you're packing raw hamburger in your purse."

Confused, Tori held up her small, black wristlet. She dangled it in front of the corgis, swung it to the left, and then the right. The dogs, however, ignored it and were still staring straight at her. Tori looked at Vance and shrugged.

"I have no idea. I didn't spill anything on me, did I?"

"Not that I can see," Vance said, shaking his head.

"Yet, you've got something they're interested in," I murmured. I caught sight of Tori's necklace and my eyebrows lifted. No. There's no way. "Tori? Could I get you to do me a huge favor?"

Tori nodded. "Of course. What can I do for you?"

"Your necklace. Where'd you get it?"

Tori looked down at the small, crystal cross she was wearing and gave it a wistful smile. "Do you like it? It's Waterford. Vance bought it for me last year."

"Waterford," I repeated. "As in, Waterford crystal, from Ireland?"

"That's a big ten-four," Vance confirmed. "Darn thing was expensive. You'll never guess how much it … but that doesn't matter, does it? The point is, I know you love everything from Ireland, and since that was Irish, it was a no-brainer, you know?"

Tori shook her head and fired off an unreadable

look at her husband. Thankfully, when she looked back at me, she was smiling.

"Would you like to see it?"

"I'll be careful," I promised. "I think *that* is what the dogs are staring at."

Tori reached behind her neck and unfastened the pendant.

"My Waterford? Why?"

Tori handed the cross to Vance, who then handed it to me. I would also like to point out that the dogs tracked the pendant as it moved from chair to chair. Passing their leashes to Vance, I stood up, gave the signal for the dogs to remain there, and slowly walked around the chairs. Sure enough, the dogs watched my progression every step of the way.

"Why would they be interested in Waterford crystal?" Tori wanted to know, as she refastened the pendant around her neck.

"Because, it's Irish," I explained, as I pulled out my phone and snapped a picture. I really don't know why I was treating the arrival of the silver chest as a case, but the dogs certainly were, so why not? "At least, that's my running theory."

"The easiest way to test that would be to find something else that came from Ireland," Vance decided. He then turned to point at the rows of tables back by Jillian's front counter. "There's Irish food over there. Already had some shepherd's pie, which was fantastic, by the way. What about that?"

Tori was nodding. "It wasn't *made* in Ireland, was it?"

Vance gave his wife a sheepish smile. "Good point."

Remembering that Jillian was wearing a thick, green Aran sweater I had bought her from an actual Irish website, I pulled out my phone.

SOMETHING STRANGE GOING ON WITH DOGS. COULD YOU COME HERE? RUNNING EXPERIMENT.

Less than thirty seconds later, Jillian was at my side. The dogs were now watching Jillian, but I didn't know if that was because they knew her better than anyone else, save myself. Well, that was easy enough to figure out.

"Zachary? Is everything all right?"

I pointed at Sherlock and Watson. "For some reason, I think they're fixating on things from Ireland. A few moments ago, they were staring at Tori. Before that, they kept watching those two sisters and the O'Sullivans."

Jillian looked down at her sweater. "Oh, because I'm wearing this, you wanted to see if they'd react. Well, they *are* watching me now. Well, Watson is. Sherlock is still looking at Tori."

Vance leaned forward, interested. He held up his glass. "I have an idea. Tori? Could you get me another soda?"

Tori looked at Vance and crossed her arms over her chest. "That's funny. Your legs don't look broken, so you can ... oh, I get it. You want to know if I walk away, would Sherlock still watch me, or would he switch to Jillian, since she'd then be closest?"

Vance nodded. "That's exactly what I'm thinking."

Nodding, Tori stood, and started to walk away.

"Ahem."

Tori spun on her heel and stared at her husband. Vance waggled the glass and offered her a goofy smile. Shaking her head, Tori snatched the glass from his outstretched hand and headed to the beverage section. Then, we all turned to see who the dogs were looking at, and that was Jillian.

"Okay, you've proven your point," Vance said. He looked up at Jillian and gave her a helpless look. "I'm just not sure what that tells us."

Tori returned a few minutes later and handed her husband his drink. "Well? Did Sherlock watch me or were they looking at Jillian?"

"They were watching Jillian," I confirmed.

Right then, the O'Sullivans wandered by again, and based on the course they were taking, were intent on refilling their drinks. As Maggie looked over at me and smiled, a thought occurred. I held up a hand, and once I was certain she was looking, beckoned her over.

"Maggie? Could I show you something? I'd like to get your take on something."

Mrs. O'Sullivan nodded. Niall appeared by his wife's side and smiled at the group at our table. Realizing no one else was offering, I sprang from my seat and held my chair out to Maggie, who smiled graciously. Jillian then did the same for Niall.

Out of the corner of my eye, I saw Tori thump Vance in the gut, and then saw my detective friend shrug helplessly.

"What would you like to show me, dear?" Maggie asked.

I pulled up the picture of the Celtic shamrock on the silver box, which I had taken on my cell and slid it across the table to her.

"Have you ever seen one of these before?"

"Of course, dear. It's a shamrock."

I heard a snicker from Vance and then watched Tori give him a second thump in the gut.

"And the style?" I prompted. "See how it appears to be a Celtic design? Like it's based on a Celtic knot?"

Maggie nodded. "What of it, dear?"

"Have you ever seen this symbol before?"

Much to my surprise, and that of everyone at the table, Maggie nodded. "I have, yes, but not for many years."

"Do you know where you saw it?" Jillian asked, as she leaned forward in her chair.

Maggie's brow furrowed. "Oh, I must be mistaken. It can't be the one I'm currently thinking about."

"Your first instinct is usually right," I urged. "If you think you've seen it before, then that means you probably have. Think, Mrs. O'Sullivan. Where would you have seen this symbol?"

Curious, Niall turned to his wife and placed a wrinkled hand over hers on the tabletop.

"This would have been many years ago," Maggie sighed. "It was in a newspaper, I believe. Yes, there was some type of article in the paper. It made Daddy so angry. That's why I remember it, I suppose."

"Her father was a very quiet and timid man," Niall explained, after Maggie had fallen silent. "To find something that could irritate him to that extent, well, at the time, it was unheard of."

"Did you see the article?" Vance asked, addressing Mr. O'Sullivan.

Maggie slid the phone to her right, so Niall could see the photograph for himself. The sleek, sophisticated, state-of-the-art communications device looked incredibly out of place in Niall's arthritic hands, but that didn't stop him from clumsily poking at the display a few times. The friendly fellow peered at the image for a few moments before shaking his head.

"It is not familiar, I'm afraid. But, I can tell you this symbol is Irish by design."

"Because of the Celtic knot woven around the inside of the shamrock?" Jillian asked.

"Kinda figured that," Vance murmured.

For the third time that night, Tori thumped him in the gut.

"That's gonna leave a mark," Vance groaned.

"Then *zip it*," Tori whispered.

"Sorry."

"Don't be sorry, be *quiet*!"

Maggie shared a conspiratorial look with Tori before reaching for the phone once more. "Isn't there technology nowadays that could see inside this chest for you?"

Vance snapped his fingers. "And we have a winner! Nice one, ma'am! Zack? We should get that chest of yours x-rayed."

I nodded glumly. "Already did, pal. I drove out to the airport in Medford, and had them send it through their scanner."

"I hadn't heard what had happened," Jillian reported. "What did they find?"

"Nothing, I'm afraid."

Jillian sighed. "It's empty? That's disappointing. I was hoping there'd be *something* in there."

"I guess I should explain," I added, drawing everyone's attention. "I had the chest x-rayed, only ..."

"Only what?" Vance asked.

"The x-ray was blank. They tried several times to get some type of image, only we saw nothing but an empty square each time it went through the scanner."

"The inside is lined with lead," Jillian whispered.

Vance nodded. "That's what I'm thinking. Oh, this keeps getting better and better! Who in the world would send you a strange Irish chest, from Wales of all places, and without a way to open it up?"

"And without a way to see inside?" Tori added.

I held up my hands in a helpless manner. I just didn't know.

Right then, another group of people wandered by our table. Sherlock and Watson scrambled to their feet and focused on one of the women. She was in her thirties, the same as the rest of the group (as near as I could tell). What, then, had caught the corgis' interest this time? As if on cue, three guys passed our table, dressed in jeans and tee shirts. The dogs immediately zeroed in on the last guy to pass us.

I honestly have no idea. I quietly snapped a few pictures and silently hoped that no one noticed I was taking pictures of passing strangers. That would take some explaining to Jillian, no doubt about it.

# FOUR

Just try to understand," the woman at the semi-circular front desk was saying, "if they make a mess in any way, shape, or form, then you will be the one responsible for cleaning it up."

I looked down at Sherlock and Watson, who both turned to look up at me.

"Perfectly understandable. Thank you for allowing them in here. I get the impression I leave them alone in my Jeep more often than I should."

"They're cute," the middle-aged woman decided. Finally, with a smile, she waved me through, as if she was a bouncer at a bar and she had finally located my name on the VIP list. "Welcome to Medford Community College library. If you have any questions, please don't hesitate to ask."

"Thanks. Most libraries have public-use computers. Do you know where I could find them? I've got some research to do."

The librarian perked up. "Oh? What kind of research, if you don't mind me asking?"

Well familiar with people asking me this question, I had five different responses primed and ready to go. Opting for the most popular, I gave the woman a smile and a wink.

"It's for a book I'm working on. I'm sorry, my publisher has forbidden me from talking about it until a month or two before its release. I hope you understand."

"If I wasn't curious before," the woman began, "then I certainly am now. Please, help yourself. You'll find the computer cubicles over there, against the eastern wall."

Thanking the matronly librarian profusely, the dogs and I headed for the closest, open work station. Signaling the dogs to stay put, I began my search. As the computer worked to tabulate the results from my query, I thought back to the events of the last two days.

Ever since learning that x-rays were ineffective against the chest, I had been doing everything in my power to try and figure out what was in it. Pomme Valley's antique expert, Burt Johnson, had assured me the box was British. He even went so far as to point out which symbols were which. Granted, the mysterious chest had all sorts of figures and images, recognizable or not, over every available surface, save the bottom. Now, the most identifiable, the shamrock, had cemented the link to Ireland.

I wanted to know why.

So, I spent the vast majority of yesterday in PV's own tiny library, hoping against hope that I'd be able to find some type of clue as to the nature of the chest. I sat at one of the library's public terminals for hours, looking at image after image of shamrocks. Did I find one that was a match for the chest? No. Did I find any books that referenced a shamrock? Yes. In fact, way too many to count, which explains the amount of time I spent digging through crammed cases, full of books. Hour after hour I searched and not one of the hundreds of shamrocks I had found was even remotely close to the one on that silver chest. What did it mean? Easy. I needed to expand my search, and that was why I was currently one town over, with my dogs in tow. I wasn't about to leave them alone in the house for a second day in a row.

After close to an hour of fruitless searching, a sense of exasperation had settled in again. Was I finding new books to read? Of course. Were there new designs to ponder? Indubitably. But, were any of the images close to what I was looking for?

No.

"Aww! What cute dogs!"

I turned at the sound of the friendly voice. This hadn't been the first time one of the college's many students had stopped by my work station to give Sherlock and Watson a friendly scratch. The owner of this particular voice was young, female, and maybe eighteen or nineteen years of age. Two other girls were directly behind her, and all of them, I might add, were laden with books.

"Hey there. How are you three doing today? Are you working on a research project?"

"The American Revolution," the first girl said, nodding her head. "Could I pet your dogs?"

"Sure. This is Sherlock and Watson. They're both..."

"...corgis!" the girl happily exclaimed.

Without waiting for permission, she set her stack of books next to my discard pile, and immediately dropped into a sitting position on the ground. Both of my dogs raced to see who could get in the girl's lap the fastest. And the winner? Watson.

"Sherlock and Watson?" the black-haired girl in the back repeated. Then, her face lit up with a smile of recognition. "I know these two! They're police dogs, aren't they?"

I shrugged. "Kinda."

"They've solved murder cases, haven't they?" a third voice incredulously asked.

"They have," I confirmed. "Go ahead and ask."

"Ask what?" the first girl wanted to know.

"You want to know if they're smarter than me? Well, the answer is a resounding yes."

This made all three girls laugh out loud, and they were promptly shushed by the same woman who had allowed the dogs access in the first place.

"What are you doing here?" the first girl said, in a hushed whisper. "Are you working a case?"

"Consider it *my* research project," I admitted. "I'm trying to track down a very specific shamrock design, and thus far, it's been eluding me."

"A shamrock?" the black-haired girl asked. "As in, Ireland?"

"Yes. Have you ever seen an intricate Celtic knot, woven into the shape of a shamrock?"

All three girls shook their heads. Then, the black-haired girl blinked a few times as, clearly, something had just occurred to her.

"You should ask the professor of my World History class. She's the smartest person I know."

"She's not a grump, is she?" I hesitantly asked. "The last time I was on this campus, and asked a professor for assistance, he turned out to be a real jerk."

All three teenagers shook their heads.

"You'll have nothing to worry about," the first teen assured me. "She's ... how would you describe her?"

"Patient," the third girl decided.

"Fair," the second teen said.

"Approachable," the first girl said, after taking a few moments to decide on the proper adjective.

"I *love* her accent!" the second teenager said, drawing grunts of affirmation from her two companions.

"Accent?" I repeated. "Er, where is she from?"

"Great Britain," the first girl answered. "Or is it

Australia? I always have a hard time distinguishing between the two of them. Anyway, if you go talk to her, then I'm sure she'll be able to help you."

I looked at the third girl, who smiled at me. She mouthed *British*, and then nudged her two friends, tapping on her watch as she did so. Right on cue, both corgis rolled to their feet, gave themselves a thorough shaking, and tugged on their leashes. And people don't think dogs can understand English? They've obviously never owned a dog before.

"Thank you, I think I will. Where can I find her?"

The girl gave me instructions on where to find the professor, and the class where she would be teaching. Bidding the trio goodbye, the dogs and I headed for the exit. This time, we were stopped only four times. Yes, you can take their pictures. No, the dogs don't have their own social media accounts. No, I'm not going to consider creating an online presence for the dogs.

What was it with the general public, anyway? Do people really put their pets online and try to get strangers interested in what they're doing? Now, before you respond to that, I will say yes, most people would be very interested in what Sherlock and Watson do on a daily basis, but there's no way I'm going to approach absolute strangers and ask them to become fans of the dogs. The dogs already have enough admirers in Pomme

Valley alone. They don't need more, thank you very much.

I'd like to say that I was able to follow the girl's directions without getting turned around, but then again, I did have to consult my notes. Somehow, Sherlock and Watson knew where I wanted to go and took the lead. Ignoring all the compliments the students heaped upon them, the dogs led me through hallways, down several flights of stairs, and past a row of identical doors, only to stop at a door that looked no different than all the others. Leaning forward, I pressed my ear to the surface. What did I hear?

Nothing. Well, nothing discernible, that is. Television shows and movies would have you believe that sound could easily travel through walls. Anyone in close proximity to a spoken discussion would easily be able to hear what was being said.

Well, I'm sorry. That's not how it happened for me. What I heard was a very muted, one-sided conversation. I could only assume that, since it was coming from the other side of the door, the history teacher I had been referred to was in the midst of some type of conversation.

Knocking politely, I waited for a few moments until I heard a woman's voice telling me to enter. The dogs and I stepped through, and found ourselves in a surprisingly large faculty office. There was a large, eight-foot-long executive's desk directly in front of the door. Book cases lined the walls, and there was a large world map with a plethora of multi-colored pins sticking out of it on the wall behind the desk. And sitting behind the desk, chatting away on the phone and completely ignoring me? A thirty-something woman with wavy brown hair currently pulled up in a ponytail. She was wearing a dark blue, long-sleeved blouse and black slacks. A laptop was on the desk, facing the owner of the desk, and a leather satchel sat on a barrel chair in the far corner.

Without making eye contact, she pointed at the chair in the corner and continued her phone call, all without a care in the world that I could overhear the conversation. I could only assume she thought I was some type of student.

"No, Lou, I'm not going to continue arguing this point. Nothing you can say will sway my mind. Now, if you want to talk about the Six Nations finals, I might be inclined to listen. Otherwise, you'll just have to accept that most people here don't care."

The girl from the library was right. British accents *are* amazing. Just listening to this professor talk, er, argue, was almost enough to make me pull out my phone and book another trip to London. Yes, I have been there before, and yes, it's just as amazing as you've heard and/or imagined.

"With that out of the way," the woman continued, "do you have any legitimate business to discuss, or are you still trying to argue your point? Argue it is. Listen, I have to go. I have someone in my office. Yes, love, until next time."

The woman placed the phone's receiver back onto the cradle on her desk, sighed, and looked up at me. She slowly rose to her feet. After a few moments, she noticed my two canine companions and a smile broke out on her face.

"Corgis! Oh, I so love the breed."

That's all Sherlock and Watson needed to hear. They would have switched to their Clydesdale personas to yank me over to the other side of the desk, but seeing how there was nowhere for them to go, and I was effectively blocking the door, I decided to let the leashes drop. In a flash, both corgis were sitting before the professor, and looking up at her with large, intelligent eyes. Sherlock even had the audacity to raise a foreleg, as if in greeting.

"Brown-nosers," I grumbled, but not before letting the woman see my smile. "Are you Professor Whyte?"

The woman shook my hand. "Call me Amanda. What can I do for you?"

For those of you familiar with my dogs, you will know what was about to happen. A certain someone did *not* like to be left out of the introductions. You'd think I would have remembered that, considering how many times I thought Sherlock had shattered an eardrum or two.

My tri-colored corgi let out a sharp, piercing bark. Sitting there, in an enclosed office, I had briefly wondered if, had Professor Whyte had a window in her office, it would have shattered. Squatting next to the dogs, I laid a friendly hand on Sherlock's back.

"Are your ears bleeding? I think mine are. Sorry. You'd think I would know not to ignore him."

"Is your dog trying to say he wants to be introduced?" Professor Whyte asked, incredulous.

"He's not a fan of being ignored. So, on my right is Sherlock, and on my left is ..."

"... Watson!" Professor Whyte exclaimed. "You three are from Pomme Valley, aren't you? I've heard all about you."

"You know me?" I asked. "I'm shocked. Most people only know my dogs."

Professor Amanda Whyte stared at me as though she was trying to see into my soul. Uh-oh. Had I said something to upset her? Then, the reason for the disquieting look became clear, and I couldn't help but smile.

"You don't, do you? You know my dogs, but you don't know me. Well, that's okay. I can forgive you for that."

"I am so sorry," Amanda began. "Please tell me, what's your name?"

"Zachary Anderson, caretaker to their Royal Canineships, Sherlock and Watson. At your service."

Professor Whyte briefly smiled at me before dropping her gaze back to the dogs. She gave each of them a thorough scratch behind their ears before turning back to me.

"Tell me, to what do I owe the pleasure of this visit? What can I do for you?"

I pulled the chair close to Professor Whyte's desk and leaned forward to rest my elbows on the walnut surface.

"What do you know about shamrocks?"

"Shamrocks? Of all the things you could have said, I wouldn't have expected you to start with that. Well, I can tell you they're a nationally recognized symbol from Ireland. Let's see. It shouldn't be confused with a four-leaf clover. It … what is your interest with shamrocks? Did you say and I missed it?"

"Have you ever seen a Celtic knot in the shape of a shamrock?" I nonchalantly asked.

Amanda stared at me a for a few moments before sinking back into her chair. "Shamrocks have been represented in a myriad of ways throughout the years. But, as a Celtic knot? Why do you ask?"

"It's a mystery I'm trying to solve," I admitted. I pulled out my cell and brought up the picture of the chest I had taken a few days ago. "What do you think?"

Professor Whyte took my phone and was silent as she studied the image. I watched her zoom in on the image, then out, and then back in. We spent the next five minutes in absolute silence as she stared at my phone. It wasn't until Watson shook her collar that the professor finally looked up.

"What is this shamrock on? Some type of box?"

"Of sorts," I answered. "I'm just trying to find out more about it, that's all."

Amanda handed me my phone, closed her eyes,

and leaned back in her chair. After a few moments, I saw the chair begin to gently rock back and forth. I detected movement coming from the ground, and after glancing at the dogs, I could see that both of them had practically fallen into a trance. The corgis were staring at Amanda, unblinking. What was going on?

"Are you okay?" I softly asked.

"Just a moment," Amanda softly returned. After a few more minutes had passed, her eyes opened and she looked over at me. Smiling, she nodded. "I'm sorry about that. Most people become completely uncomfortable whenever I am quiet for that long."

"What were you doing?"

"It's a type of memory exercise. You see, I remember seeing a very unique shamrock, much like the one you had just shown me, only it was many years ago. What do you know about *Method of Loci*?"

"I'm not sure. Is it some type of memory exercise?"

"It's a memorization technique commonly known as *Memory Palace*, which is something an old friend taught me years ago."

Unsure what this had to do with shamrocks, I politely smiled and nodded.

"I could take the next four hours and teach you all about how to build your own memory palace, but suffice to say, I have one, and it's how I manage to remember things. That shamrock? I have seen it. I was just looking at it. It was in an old book I found in the library at the University of London."

"What do you remember about it?"

Amanda's eyes closed again. After a few minutes, she began to speak. "The reference is old, at least a hundred years or older. Your shamrock spent nearly two months on the front page of the local newspaper. However, try as I might, I can't read the article. That means I never read it in the first place."

"You said *local*," I recalled. "What is considered local to you?"

A few more moments of silence passed. "County Dublin."

"Ireland," I whispered. "So, the chest is tied to something that happened a hundred years ago, in Ireland, but what?"

Amanda's eyes opened and they cleared. She then reached for her satchel, retrieved a tablet computer, and began furiously tapping the screen. After only a few moments, she let out a triumphant shout and slid the tablet over to me.

"I *knew* I had seen it before."

I was looking at a picture of a yellowing newspaper, brittle with age, that had been preserved in a book. The edges were cracked, and chunks of the paper had evidently crumbled away, but the vast majority of the article was present, only it was too tiny to read. Attempts at zooming in on the picture only resulted in a photograph too pixelated to be able to read. Directly in the center of the photograph was a very familiar symbol. It was, without a shadow of a doubt, the same shamrock. It was the same shape, the same orientation, and the same design. The image of the shamrock had been enlarged. To make absolutely certain, I pulled back up the photograph of the chest on my phone and compared the shamrocks.

Identical.

"What book is this?" I wanted to know.

"I'm sorry, it doesn't say. The one bit I *can* make out is that it was printed in 1983."

"That's not what I was expecting," I admitted, as I studied the picture.

Amanda leaned around me to zoom out the picture on her tablet. While the picture of the shamrock remained, since the photo only depicted the three-leafed sprig, I was now able to see what was written next to the picture. What I saw had my eyes widening with surprise and me stifling a curse.

### IRISH CROWN JEWELS STOLEN! INSIDE JOB SUSPECTED!

Looking back at the professor, I tapped the article.

"Is this for real?"

"It was the unsolved mystery of the century," Amanda told me. "Still is. Those jewels were never recovered."

"What happened? How could someone have stolen such famous jewels?"

"You do understand that the security systems back in the turn of the century were nothing compared to what we have today?"

"Yeah, true, but I still find it unlikely. Do they know who took the jewels?"

Amanda was shaking her head. "They suspected it was an inside job."

"I can't help but notice you didn't have to look that fact up," I pointed out. "How is it you know about this stuff?"

"As if you couldn't tell from my accent," Amanda began, with a smile, "I'm British. The theft of those jewels is part of our history. Every school child learns about it at an early age."

"Can you tell me what happened? Better yet, when did it happen?"

"It was 1907. The security of the jewels had been entrusted to the Ulster King of Arms, Sir Arthur Vicars. Vicars, it was said, was rather lax with his security."

"What happened?" I asked.

"The jewels were kept in Dublin Castle and were guarded by the Ulster King of Arms and a 24-hour outdoor patrol of soldiers and policemen. A saferoom was built in 1903, but in an ironic twist of fate, it was revealed that the safe that stored the jewels was too big to fit inside the safe room. Therefore, the safe remained outside the strongroom, in the library.

"There were two keys to the safe," Amanda continued. "Vicars kept one locked away, in his desk at home."

"And the other was stolen, wasn't it?" I guessed.

"No. Vicars was a little forgetful. There are stories that he would have a little too much to drink, and those keys ended up with his friends."

"That probably didn't go over too well."

"It didn't. But, on July 6, 1907, a maid assigned to Belford Tower discovered the door to the safe-room open. The bolt to the inner door was locked, but the key to open the lock was left in the door it-self. Vicars didn't think much of this, and it wasn't until later in the day that he discovered the safe had been cleaned out, the jewels stolen."

"Didn't they look for them?" I asked.

Professor Whyte nodded. "Dublin Metropol-itan launched an investigation, but sadly, the jewels were never recovered. As I said, everyone figured it was an inside job."

"Vicars," I said, after a few moments.

"He denied it every waking moment. And do you know what? I'm actually inclined to believe him."

Was *that* what was waiting for me inside that silver chest? Missing, *stolen* jewelry of extreme historical importance? If so, why in the world would someone send them to me? What was I sup-posed to do with them? I mean, if it turned out those jewels were in there, and I could find a way to open the chest, then you had better believe I would be sending those things straight back to Ire-land!

My eyes widened as I remembered what I had left sitting on my coffee table back home. Had I really left the Irish Crown Jewels so exposed? It was time to cut this meeting short.

"Well, I do thank you for your time," I said.

"Mr. Anderson," Professor Whyte formally began, "do you have the Irish Crown Jewels in your possession?"

"Honestly? I have no idea. I sincerely doubt it. But, I will make you this promise. If those jewels happen to be in my possession, then I will do everything in my power to get them returned to their rightful owners. Fair enough?"

Amanda slipped me a business card. "Fair enough. Do keep me apprised, would you? I'm sure Her Majesty, the Queen of England, would love to have that particular mystery solved."

Thanking the professor for her time, I hurried the dogs out of the college and back to the Jeep.

"They couldn't possibly be in there," I mumbled, as I sped home. "And if they are? Who in their right flippin' mind would send them to me? I had nothing to do with the theft. Talk about it being *waaayyy* before my time."

The dogs watched me in the rearview mirror. Sherlock was staring at me as though he couldn't believe he was now associated with a thief.

"I didn't do it," I told the corgi. "Stop looking at me as though I did, okay?"

Pulling up to the winery, I threw the Jeep in park, helped each of the dogs to the ground, and hurried inside. I was honestly expecting to find a ransacked house, with cabinets open, junk strewn about, and furniture upended, or destroyed. But no, everything was just as I left it. And there, sitting out on the coffee table for everyone to see, including having a great line of sight to the window overlooking the porch, was the silver chest. I noticed the shamrock glinting in the sunlight as I approached.

"What am I going to do with this thing?" I asked no one in particular. "Where should I stash it?"

My first instinct was to call up some of my friends. Perhaps one of them could suggest something that no one else would think of? However, even before I could pull my phone from my pocket, I hesitated. If I did involve Harry or Vance, then that could theoretically put them in danger. And Jillian? Forget about it. There was no way I was going to place her in harm's way.

I snapped my fingers as an idea formed. "A bank safety deposit box. It'd be safe there."

Just as quickly, I dismissed the notion. It would take too long to set up. I needed to get rid of this thing, like *yesterday*.

I looked at the chest and sighed. Someone had given it to me, so I could only assume someone wanted me to do the right thing. That had to be returning it to its rightful owners, didn't it? I had to find a way to open this chest. Somewhere, somehow, there was a solution. I just needed more time to figure it out, and that meant I had to hide the box, but where?

"Come on, guys. Help me out, would you? You find all kinds of things. Fine. Where would be a great place to stash this thing?"

The dogs were up to the task. Just like that, Sherlock and Watson ran to the door, wanting to be let outside. Unfortunately for me, in the frame of mind I was in, I thought someone was approaching the house.

"What? What do you hear? Help me hide this thing! Hurry!"

Both dogs turned to look at me as though I, once more, bore the moniker of stupidest human on two legs.

"What? Stop looking at me like that. I don't want to get caught with the box. We need to secure it somewhere, but where?"

"Awwooooo wooooooooooowooo!" Sherlock howled.

Watson yipped twice, the high-pitched kind which makes you think someone had stepped on her. Familiar with my two dogs, I could tell they wanted to show me something. Flashing my dogs the time-out gesture, as though they knew what it meant, I took the stairs two at a time as I hurried to the master bedroom. Rushing into the closet, I grabbed the closest bag I could find and sprinted back down the stairs.

Unzipping the small, black duffel bag, and grunting with satisfaction after I saw that it was a perfect fit for the silver chest, I followed the dogs outside, curious as to what they were going to do. I could only hope some intruder wasn't hiding out there, ready to conk me over the head and steal the chest at the first opportunity.

Sherlock and Watson ran up the hill, behind the main house. They were headed to the winery? Could I find a decent spot to hide the chest there? I suppose there was enough machinery to …

Sherlock deftly navigated around the winery and headed toward the newest building on the property, which was the fairly recently completed warehouse. Thanks to Caden and his future plans for the winery, we had planted an orchard, including apple, pear, cherry, and several other types of trees. There were also several varieties of berry bushes. Wine can be made from fruit other than grapes, my winemaster had informed me, but, if we wanted to try it, then we were going to need a place to age the wine, since fruit-based wine took longer to prepare. Hence, the new warehouse.

The dogs ran to the front door and waited for the person who sounded—and probably looked—like a lumbering hippo to catch up. Fumbling for my keys, we entered the vast warehouse and navigated our way through the two sets of double doors until we entered the main storage facility. Aside from the seriousness of the situation, I couldn't help but nod and give Caden a silent high-five. The efficient vintner was already making use of the space. At first glance, I could see five or six rows of ten barrels each on either side of the long hallway. Granted, in the overall scheme of things, this was less than a tenth of the overall space. However, an idea had dawned. My question was, how the hell had the dogs thought of it first?

I pulled my bag over to a stack of empty barrels. Looking at the black duffel, and the silver chest it contained, I nodded at the dogs and started the work necessary to secure the chest. In this case, I pulled on a set of work gloves and rolled an empty barrel off the nearest rack and maneuvered it in place, next to a whole slew of full barrels. Carefully placing the disguised chest inside, I sealed the barrel with its lid and carefully stepped back to study my work.

It was perfect.

I allowed myself a brief moment to appreciate the situation. Have you ever seen *Raiders of the Lost Ark*? And—spoiler alert—after they recover the missing ark, do you remember the government officials stashing the prize in a crate? That crate was then placed in an enormous warehouse with similar crates, effectively hiding the ark in plain sight. That was, in effect, what was happening here. Granted, there were significantly fewer barrels than there were crates in the movie, but unless you knew that one of those barrels contained the shamrock chest, you'd never know it was there.

That, to me, was the perfect hiding place. Patting each dog on the head, we made our way out of

the warehouse, stopping only long enough to lock
the door.

## FIVE

A re you really not going to try it? I'm telling you, buddy, it's still the same. All they've done is add a few drops of food coloring."

"No offense, pal," I hotly began, as I held up my mug and stared at the frothy contents it contained, "but there's no way I can drink this. I don't know how many times I have to say it, but if the beer looks like what the Joker took a bath in, then it is *not* goin' anywhere near my mouth."

In response, Vance took his own mug and drank nearly half of his holiday-themed beverage. He smacked his lips and held his tankard aloft. "Ahh. That's what a body needs after a long day. You're seriously not going to drink that? What, don't you trust this place? Isn't Casa de Joe's your favorite restaurant?"

I slid my own beer over to him and ordered my

usual. In a bottle, thank you very much. The wait-ress smiled, nodded, and headed back inside the restaurant. Yes, we were out on the pet-friendly terrace, and yes, I had Sherlock and Watson with me. I'm not sure what sort of frolicking the two of them did last night after I turned off the lights, but today? They've been napping pretty much the en-tire day.

"What have you been working on?" I asked. I heard Sherlock snoring from below the table and reached down to give each dog a pat. "Do you need help with anything?"

"Just a rash of car thefts," Vance reported. He sighed and stared into the depths of his drink. "It's odd, though. People don't generally steal sports cars and then stick around the area."

Surprised, I looked at my friend. "You know these stolen cars are still in the area, but we haven't been able to catch the guy responsible?"

"No. Just earlier today, a 2011 Dodge Challen-ger was reported missing from its owner's garage. Toxic orange."

"Those cars are so cool," I sighed. "I love the retro muscle car feel to them. Reminds me of the Challenger we had when we were in Phoenix. Did you say toxic orange? Is that the color? Cool name for a paint color, amigo. Hey, does this orange one have the extra power?"

"If you're asking whether or not it's a Challen-ger Hellcat, then no, it is not. This one only had 350 horsepower under the hood."

"*Only* has 350 horsepower," I mocked, as I let out another groan. "My Jeep? Nowhere near that. Someday, I'll get something with a lot of power."

"You're getting married," Vance reminded me. "No, you're not."

"Say the word, and I can get the dogs involved. You know how good Sherlock and Watson are at finding things."

I heard the snoring pause momentarily and I'm assuming that, since neither of us moved from the table, was why the snoring resumed. A quick check confirmed both corgis were still out cold.

"If I need their help, I'll let you know," Vance promised. "All right, you wanted to meet for lunch out here. What's on your mind?"

Grinning at my friend, I reached for the padded envelope sitting on the chair next to me, which was below the level of the table, so Vance couldn't see it. Placing it directly before me, I then pushed it toward Vance, who frowned when he saw it.

"What's this?"

"Something I thought you'd like to see."

"Oh?" Vance pried open the metal fastener and opened the package.

A thick, glossy paperback slid into his hands. I watched as Vance turned the book over in his hands, so he could see the cover. I waited nearly twenty seconds to get some type of reaction out of him, but no, I was denied. Instead, Vance handed it back to me.

"I'm not much of a reader, pal," my detective

friend began, "but thanks anyway."

I pushed the book back into his hands. "You really ought to give this one a try."

"Why's that?"

"Well, what do you see on the cover?"

The cover was studied once more.

"Well, it's green, so wherever this is supposed to depict, it clearly rains there."

"Spot on so far. What else do you see?"

Vance's gaze dropped to a lone figure, a red-haired woman, standing before a simple thatched cottage. Pens were nearby, with cattle and horses seen grazing on the lush green grass. A gray tendril escaped from the cottage's chimney and lazily rose into the sky.

That's when I saw my friend's eyes widen. He stared at the female figure, took note of the color of her hair, and then stared at the scenery behind the house, which depicted rolling green hills, complete with stone fences. And, I'm quite thrilled to add, his mouth dropped open.

"Is ... is this yours?"

I nodded. Vance then tapped the author's name. "Jim McGee? Isn't this supposed to be your name?"

"It's an experiment," I admitted. "I don't have my actual name on anything. Chastity Wadsworth is the only name I've used, but that's for romance novels. This one isn't a romance, and it's set in Ireland, so I thought an Irish-sounding name would be better."

"How would you be able to tell if it's better?" Vance asked, bewildered. "I trust you, pal. You clearly know what you're doing, so if you're happy, I'm happy. Wow. So, this is the book? *Feeding the Flames*, by Jim McGee. It looks ..."

"What?" I inquired. "Do you see something wrong?"

"No, it's just that ... I have no words. Thanks, buddy. Think it'll sell?"

My smile was back, which didn't go unnoticed by Vance.

"What's that look for? Do you think it will?"

"I *know* it will," I confirmed. "And if you don't believe me, that's fine. You can take the word from my publisher, who has said the preorders alone are breaking records left and right."

"People are preordering this?" Vance asked, as he waggled the book in front of me.

"By the thousands," I informed him. "At last count, nearly 30,000 people had ordered the book through one of their favorite retailers."

"How?" Vance demanded. "You said it was a preorder. And this pseudonym of yours is brand new?"

"It is," I said, nodding. I already knew where my friend was going with this, and was anxiously awaiting his arrival.

"So, if this is not available yet," Vance continued, "and you've never used this name before, then how are you getting the word out? How do people know it's any good?"

"Editors and beta readers."

"Huh?"

"My editors. They've already read it, given feedback, and allowed their pool of beta readers access to it. Every single beta reader, and I do mean every one of 'em, absolutely loved the story. Let's see if I can remember some of the comments. One said she loved the protagonist, and how fiercely independent she was. Another loved the Irish setting. Trust me, the list goes on and on."

I could see Vance's mouth moving, which meant he was working on figuring out the math involved. After a few moments, Vance looked over at me.

"Umm, how much …"

"How much money do we get from each sale?" I finished for him.

Vance slowly nodded.

"Most traditionally published authors get between 8-10%. As for me, well, my publisher likes me, so I get 30%. Since this is a story based on Tory, then I'll be splitting that with you, fifty-fifty."

"But … that means …"

"Yeah, that's exactly what it means," I said, correctly guessing what was going through my friend's brain. "The ebook is selling for $9.99. That means we'll make about $3 per sale. You heard me mention how many preorders there had been, right? Thirty thousand? The math says that you and I just made over $13,000, and that's in the first two weeks, pal."

"How?" Vance demanded. "What ...? How could you ...? I ... I ... I don't understand. How do people even know to order it? How do they even know it exists?"

"Because I've got a damn good publisher," I answered. "Let me just say that they earn every penny of their cut. They're good at marketing and promotions, so let's just let them keep doing what they're doing."

"How many more people will be ordering this?" Vance incredulously asked.

I shrugged. "Who can say? If it was up to the publisher, and, in this case, it is, then they're going to try and get as many sales as possible."

"Wow. Tori is gonna freak out. What are we going to do with that much money? I mean, I guess I should let Tori know."

I reached for my beer and finished it off. I also noticed Vance's was gone, too. I caught the wait-ress' eye and held up my bottle. She promptly nod-ded, and headed toward the bar.

"Can I make a suggestion?"

"Sure, pal."

"No, Vance, I mean, may I make a very serious suggestion and let it be something I strongly hope you do?"

"What's that?"

"Take Tori to Ireland. You will have enough to take her on a First Class trip to the Emerald Isle. Trust me when I say, the country is even more amazing than all the movies and television shows lead you to believe. She'll love it. You will love it."

"Ireland," Vance said, as he nodded. "That would be one mother of a surprise, wouldn't it?"

"It would. Would you take the girls?"

"What do you think?" Vance asked.

"Let me ask you this," I countered. "When was the last time just you and Tori did something for yourselves? When was the last time you two had some quality time to be together?"

"Since before Tiffany was born," Vance scoffed. "Why?"

"I'd say that answers your question. Give yourself two weeks. See if you can get Tori's parents to watch the girls. If they can't, then call me. Jillian and I can watch them."

Vance fell silent as he studied me for a few moments. Then, he held up his fist, which I gave a solid bump with my own.

"Are you sure you wouldn't want to come with us?"

"Tempting," I admitted. "However, I've already told Jillian that we'll be honeymooning in Ireland, and that'll be in September of this year."

"What if ... what if we came with you? I mean, I know it's your honeymoon, but what would you say to the four of us exploring the country together?"

The waitress arrived with another round of drinks.

"Are you sure you don't want to explore Ireland

on your own?" I asked. "If you're worried about getting lost, you can join a tour group and let someone else do all the driving and planning."

"What are you guys going to do? Has Jillian ever been there before?"

"She hasn't, no. Since I have, I thought it'd be more fun to explore on our own."

"See? That's what I want to do."

"Are you sure? There is something to be said for only being responsible for showing up. That's what I did the first time I was there. We took a tour of Cork via bus, and then in Dublin, the same thing. I loved Cork, and seeing the colorful row homes running along the waterfront. I loved seeing the countryside, visiting Blarney Castle, and shopping at Blarney Woollen Mills."

"I want to do that, too."

"Then, you should take a tour. As for us? Well, I've always been fond of the small, quaint Irish villages, and the majority of 'em are on the western side of the island."

"I get it," Vance said, growing sober as his excitement faded. "You and Jillian should be alone."

"No! I'm sorry, man. That's not what I'm saying. I personally have no problems having you guys with us. Experiencing Ireland is something everyone should be able to do in their lifetime. This is the perfect opportunity for you guys to do just that. Tell you what. Let me talk to Jillian."

"Just promise me that, should Jillian say no, that you'll just say so, okay? I don't want to get in the way of you two."

"No worries, amigo. No worries."

A cricket chirped loudly nearby. Being famil-iar with me and my penchant for insectoid alert tones, Vance pointed at my phone.

"That was you, buddy. Seriously, man, you ought to change that tone to something more friendly."

"If I change it out now, then I'll never know when someone is texting me, or the phone is try-ing to get my attention."

"Your phone just alerted you to something, and yet you still didn't know what happened," Vance pointed out.

"Yeah, yeah. Let's see what we have."

"Missed text message?" Vance guessed. "I'll bet Jillian just texted you, didn't she?"

I stared at the image on my phone and felt the color drain out of my face. I should also point out that both dogs were suddenly wide awake and on their feet. Concerned, Vance scrambled to his feet and rushed up behind me so he could look over my shoulder, at my phone. What he saw had him swearing like a sailor.

It was a notification from my security cameras. Someone had just walked up my front porch and was standing in front of my door. Then, I watched —in real time—as the man wearing dark cam-ouflage produced a black zippered pouch. It was opened, revealing rows of tools on either flap of the pouch.

Anyone who has ever seen a television show, or a movie, knew what had just happened. The person standing at my door had just pulled out a set of lock picks. Just like that, my door opened, and the man slipped inside.

"Can he not see the cameras?" Vance asked, as we hurriedly paid the bill and raced to the restaurant's parking lot.

"They're tiny. Plus, I've hidden them in obscure locations. Here, hold this, would you?"

I passed my phone to Vance as I scooped up the dogs and placed them in the back seat.

"Didn't you say you were being followed by someone in a black Mercedes?" my detective friend suddenly asked.

"What about it?"

Vance held the phone out so that I could see the display. Apparently, Vance had found the option on the app that would toggle between the various feeds. The one we were looking at now was showing my driveway. There, parked near the street, was a black Mercedes Benz, complete with tinted windows.

"How certain are you that your guys found every bug?" I asked, as I sped back to my home.

"Positive," Vance answered, as he kept his eyes glued on my phone. "What system is this? I like how you're able to look through your cameras using just your phone."

"Most systems are like that," I told my friend, as I deftly swerved around cars that were on the street. "I'd really like to catch this jerk in the act of breaking into my house, but that isn't going to work if he can see us coming, or can listen in to us."

"They found one other bug on yours," Vance recalled, "and two on mine. That's when they checked the rest of the cars, including the patrol cars."

"Oh? You didn't tell me that part. What did they find?"

"Not a thing. Looks like the only two cars that were bugged were ours. Still think this is about that chest?"

"Without a doubt. I think you were bugged because you're friends with me. Hey, do me a favor, would you? Would you have someone contact Harry and have his car checked out? We already know Julie's car is clean."

"I'm on it."

Ten minutes later, as we neared the winery, I eased my foot off the accelerator. For anyone who lived in the country like this, the approach of a car could be heard from nearly a mile away. Feeling a tap on my shoulder, I saw that Vance was pointing at a turnout on my right, about a hundred feet up the road. That meant Lentari Cellars was less than a quarter of a mile away. In fact, we were now driving along my property, seeing how we were now passing acre after acre of prime farmland, and the only thing that was growing was row after row of vines.

Stashing the Jeep on the side of the road, the

dogs and I took off after Vance, who had drawn his sidearm. As soon as we made it to the entrance of my driveway, Vance whipped his own cell out and took several pics of the sleek, black sedan waiting just inside a row of hedges, making it practically invisible from the road. Vance hurried around to the rear of the vehicle and took a picture of the license plate and then, thinking it couldn't hurt, snapped a pic of the car's VIN.

"You two need to be quiet," I whispered to the dogs. "No barking, okay? We want to catch this guy red-handed."

Both dogs craned their necks to look up at me. As if that was all they needed to hear, both Sherlock and Watson pulled on their leashes, anxious to resume moving. Neither, I might add, made the tiniest bit of sound. How they knew we needed to approach in stealth was beyond me. However, that *almost* changed as we neared my front porch.

Sherlock looked up the short flight of steps, toward the front door, and started to gently sway from side to side. I recognized the behavior almost immediately. The tri-colored corgi was agitated, presumably by the fact that both Vance and I had halted near the porch steps. Sure, we were trying to figure out if the guy was still in the house, but I could see that Sherlock was about to start arguing with me.

"No, you don't," I whispered, as I dropped into a squat next to him. "Quiet, pal, okay? No howling. Is he up there?"

Sherlock only had eyes for the front door. Vance, holding his sidearm in his right hand, signaled for me to stay put. He edged up the stairs, poked his head through the open door, and then looked back at me.

"The door is open, and the place is trashed," my friend reported. "I can't hear anything in there."

"He could be hiding," I pointed out, and then nodded at the dogs. "They seem to think there's someone in … guys? What now? You don't want to look in the house?"

Both Sherlock and Watson were on the move, and were headed away from the house, straight to the winery. But, the closer we got, the more Sherlock became agitated once more. Looking at the corgis, I could see that Watson wanted to go to the winery, but Sherlock acted as though he wanted to keep going. What did that mean? Then, it dawned on me. There wasn't one intruder, but two! So, what else was that way?

Only a large, freakin' building where I had happened to stash a silver chest.

Handing Sherlock's leash to Vance, I pointed at the winery, then at myself and the warehouse. Reaching into my pocket, I pulled out my keyring and unclipped a smaller set. Handing them to Vance, I pointed at the key with the green plastic ring around the head. My friend nodded, turned on his heel, and hurried over to the door.

I had just taken a few steps toward the newly constructed warehouse when I heard Sherlock bark and sounds of a struggle. While I weighed the desire to help a friend, and make darn certain nothing happened to one of my dogs, Watson suddenly surged forward, intent on getting inside the warehouse as soon as possible.

Trusting Vance to deal with whatever was going on inside the winery, I let Watson lead me over to the warehouse. Dropping down into a crouch, I used the light from my phone to inspect the locks on the door. Well, if it had been picked, then whoever had done the deed was definitely a pro. I didn't see any of the telltale scratches that are typically found whenever an amateur is the one who is doing the picking.

The warehouse door was unlocked and pushed open. The creaking noise alone could have woken the dead. Scowling, and promising whatever deities existed that I'd purchase a case of WD-40 if all the flippin' noise would just shut up, Watson and I made our way inside.

I held a finger to my lips, as though my little girl knew what that meant, as the two of us crept through the open warehouse, careful to avoid pallets, empty barrels, and pieces of shelving that were waiting to be assembled. Was there someone hiding in here? If so, it was going to take a while to search, seeing how the light from my phone could only illuminate so much.

That's when Watson pulled me to the closest wall and promptly sat. Why? Well, the little darling was staring up, at a white rectangular plate with a bank of switches on them. The little booger was no doubt wondering why I wasn't turning on the lights.

"Nobody saw that," I whispered to Watson, as I grinned at her. Watson's long tongue flopped out and she panted contentedly. "There might be someone in here. What do you say we find 'em?"

Watson rose to her feet and lowered her nose to the ground. After a few moments, she moved off, heading toward the far northern wall. Consequently, that was where the completed shelving had been installed. It also meant *that* was the direction to go in order to find the false barrel with the shamrock chest hidden inside it. No one knew it was here, so how the heck did they know to look in my new storage facility? Was it the logical place to stash something?

There was a commotion on my right. I knew exactly what it was, because I've made that same noise on more than one occasion: someone had knocked over one of the wooden barrels. An empty one, yes, but nevertheless, the noise was distinct. Since those barrels were everywhere, it was easy to misjudge where they were.

"I know you're in here, pal," I began, raising my voice so I knew it'd be heard. "You might as well give it up. You're not going to make it out of here."

"You have no idea who you're dealing with," a sinister voice returned. "Give it up. You may yet get out of this with your life."

"Give what up?" I asked. "What are you looking

for? I don't know where you got your information, pal, but whatever you're looking for, you won't find it here."

Not true, since I knew exactly what he wanted to get his hands on, but I wasn't about to tell him that, was I?

"You don't expect me to believe that, do you?" the voice sneered. "Give it up, Mr. Anderson. You don't want to make an enemy of us."

There was something about the voice that made me think this was nothing more than a bluff. There was a sense of fear behind the voice. Whoever was talking had not been expecting me to return home so soon. They did know that the bugs they had planted on my car had been neutralized, didn't they?

"Why are you so surprised, pal?" I casually asked. "You did know I was headed home, didn't you? I mean, I would have thought that you'd have left a lookout after losing contact with my car."

The intruder said nothing.

"Come on. You guys are supposed to be scary as hell! You're insinuating you're my worst nightmare. Right now, the only thing you are is an unpleasant nap. So, here's what we'll do. Go ahead and surrender. I can put in a good word for you with the local police. Perhaps we can work out some type of deal?"

"This is your last chance, Mr. Anderson. Give us the chest and we will leave you alone. Fail to do so and there will be consequences."

Yes, there it was. The voice was quavering. Whoever speaking was truly nervous. And why shouldn't they be? They were in my house, on my property, in my town. I definitely had the advantage. Perhaps it was time to use it?

"So, what's it gonna be, pal? You made a mistake coming in here. This is my winery's storage facility. There's only one way in and out of here, and you're on the wrong side of the building. There's no way out for you. The police are on the way, and if they have to search the premises to find you, I'm not gonna lift a finger to help you."

While that little spiel wasn't exactly true, since there were no fewer than four large loading doors scattered around the warehouse, the intruder didn't know that. But, I wasn't lying, either. Not only were the police on the way, they were already here. I could only hope Vance had apprehended the other guy.

Worry for Sherlock, and my friend, let's not forget that, had me anxious to wrap things up in here. Mr. Sinister Voice was in here, somewhere, and based on the commotion he had made earlier, I had a pretty good idea where he was hiding: the empty barrel racks. The north side of the facility held the filled barrels, but the northeastern corner held the *empties*, as Caden called them.

Right then, a notion occurred. I knew exactly how I was going to catch my unwanted friend.

"I don't want to kill you, Mr. Anderson," Shady Dude began, "but I ... I will if I have to."

And now he's hesitating. Yep, as amusing as this whole scenario was, I had more pressing concerns to deal with.

"Last chance, buddy," I announced, as I quietly snuck over to the empty barrels and clasped the three-foot long wooden lever at the bottom corner of the *empties* storage racks.

To best explain what I was about to do, I need to describe how my empties were stored. There was a gently sloping tier system of barrels, where if the barrel closest to the ground is used, meaning it's pulled from the line, then the barrels will roll forward, and the empty space is transferred up the line. I always said the rolling system Caden designed looked a lot like the ramps Jumpman runs up while battling Donkey Kong.

Yes, I play too many video games.

At the bottom of the ramps, there was a release lever which would allow the bottom-most barrel to be lifted from the track. Then, the next would roll forward, to take its place, and if the lever wasn't reapplied, then that barrel would simply roll off, into open air. Think of a coin-operated soda machine, and the manual release lever.

"All right, sport. Don't say I didn't warn you."

"Ooooooo!" Watson howled.

Surprised, I looked down at my little girl and grinned. Watson typically didn't howl. She let her packmate handle that department. In this case, since he was absent, she decided to voice her enthusiasm. At least, I *think* that's what she was doing.

"Bombs away."

I pulled the lever. The entire eastern wall started trembling as barrel after barrel was ejected from the storage ramps, and without the brake lever to keep them in check, they all rushed forward, one right after the other. A series of loud crashing sounds began as each empty made contact with the ground below, and what's more, the crashes increased in frequency as each barrel removed from the line picked up speed.

"Aaauuggghh!"

"Yeah, that'll probably leave a mark. Sorry 'bout that. I did warn you, didn't I?"

Pulling the lever back to the locking position, I felt the ramps shudder as the collective weight of about a dozen empty barrels clanged to a stop. Slowly walking around the corner, I peered out from behind a double-row of filled wine barrels and got my first look at Shady Dude. Well, make that the *lower* half.

It looked like the first barrel had landed directly on the intruder's head, knocking him to the ground. But, before he could regain his feet, barrels two and three came crashing down, followed thereafter by nearly a half-dozen more. Therefore, all I saw were Shady Dude's legs, jutting out from under several smashed empties.

"I suppose we should go tell Vance," I amiably told Watson.

The red and white corgi wriggled with excitement.

# SIX

Are you still upset your guy got away? Let it go, pal. We have this guy, and that's only because I dropped nearly a dozen empty wine barrels on him."

"That accounts for his broken leg," Vance conceded. "Still, I should have been able to catch the guy."

"How *did* he manage to get away? The Mercedes was still in the driveway when the police arrived."

"I'm not sure," Vance admitted. "I did hear something in the distance, after Sherlock alerted me he had doubled back and made it outside."

"What did you hear?" I asked. "Another car?"

"Motorcycle," Vance decided. "He must have had one stashed in the trees. Might explain why we didn't see it as we pulled up?"

I shrugged. It was possible. We both turned our

attention to the man with his leg in a cast, sitting handcuffed to the bar bolted onto the table. It was Shady Dude, and if I didn't know any better, I'd say he was about to turn on the waterworks. Now that I had a good chance to look at him, he looked to be in his early sixties, had short gray hair, and seemed to be in decent shape. And, I'd like to add there wasn't a single intimidating thing about him.

Vance tapped me on the shoulder and then headed out of the observation room. Following closely, he led me down the hall and into a room I hadn't been in before, which was a large conference room. Captain Nelson was already there, seated at the head of the table. On his left was a middle-aged lady who I recognized almost immediately: Debra Campbell, mayor of Pomme Valley.

The two of them looked up as we entered. Thankfully, the mayor had a smile for me, while the captain simply nodded. Mayor Campbell rose to her feet as we approached, which prompted the captain to do the same. Once the two of us were seated, Mayor Campbell resumed sitting.

"Hello, Mr. Anderson," the mayor said.

"Ma'am. How are you today?"

"Quite well, thank you. It has come to my attention that you are in possession of some type of chest?"

I nodded. "I am."

"Could you tell us about it?"

"Sure. I came home a few nights ago to find a wooden crate on my doorstep. The dogs seemed to indicate it was harmless, so I brought it inside and opened it up."

"What was in it?" the mayor curiously asked.

"A silver chest. It has markings all over it. A shamrock on one side, a thistle on the other, and a cross on another."

"Three symbols," Mayor Campbell softly repeated. "The chest is British?"

"That is what we think, too," I said. "Burt explained it to us."

"Mr. Johnson, from the antique store?" Captain Nelson asked.

I nodded. "Yes. I should also inform you that, for all intents and purposes, this chest doesn't have a lid."

Mayor Campbell looked up, interested. "No lid? Indeed. And you say it's covered with markings and symbols?"

"Every square inch," I confirmed.

"It's a puzzle box," the mayor decided.

"How so?" Captain Nelson asked.

"You have to prove yourself worthy," Mayor Campbell explained. "Solve the puzzle, and the chest opens, so you can claim the prize. Am I right to understand this particular prize might have some value?"

"If it's what we think it is," Vance began, "then yes, it's worth a pretty penny. If word got out that something like this was in Pomme Valley, then we'd have every thief in the area rushing to our city."

"Why?" the captain demanded. "What's so important? What is it you think you have?"

"The Irish Crown Jewels," I answered.

Both of the captain's bushy eyebrows jumped with surprise.

"Is that even a thing?" Captain Nelson wanted to know, as he looked to the mayor for an answer. "I've heard of the British Crown Jewels, of course. I know they're in London. I didn't know Ireland had some, too."

"Only a few pieces," Vance said, as he pulled out his notebook and flipped a few pages. Settling on one, he began to read. "Stolen in 1907, the jewels consist of a star decorated with Brazilian diamonds, a diamond badge, and five gold-and-jewel-encrusted collars."

"How big are they?" I asked. "Could they fit in that chest?"

"They were last seen over 100 years ago, pal," Vance reminded me. "I have no idea. Most jewelry is small, so if I had to venture a guess, then I'd say it was possible."

"And you're in possession of this chest now?" Captain Nelson asked.

I nodded. "Unfortunately, yes."

"And you have no idea who sent it?" Mayor Campbell asked.

"We were able to get some information off the shipping invoice," Vance announced, as he flipped through a few more pages in his notebook. "Cwmbran, a small town in Wales."

"That's where it was shipped from?" Captain Nelson asked.

I nodded, and then shrugged.

"Do you know anyone living in that town?" the mayor asked.

"I don't, I'm sorry."

Captain Nelson seemed to make up his mind about something and he nodded. Then, pushing himself away from the table, he rose to his feet, prompting the rest of us to do the same.

"What do you say we go talk to our guest? We've given him long enough to stew."

"Do keep me posted, Dale," the mayor said, as she turned to go. "Detective Samuelson. Mr. Anderson."

"Ma'am," Vance returned.

Once the mayor was gone, the three of us headed back through the hall and into the interrogation room. My friend from yesterday glared at me as I took one of the three chairs set up on the opposite side of the table.

"Don't look at me like that," I said to Shady Guy, as I sat down. "I tried to get you to surrender. I told you that pursuing this was a bad idea."

Shady Guy's lips narrowed as he frowned harder.

"Let's start with your name," Vance began, as he flipped open the police report and started to read. When several seconds of silence had passed, and there wasn't a response, my detective friend looked up. "We've already taken your fingerprints.

It's just a matter of time before you're identified. Are you sure you don't want to save yourself some trouble?"

"Any status on those prints?" Captain Nelson asked, without looking at anyone in particular.

After a few moments, there was a knock at the door and a familiar uniformed officer appeared. Officer Jones, a tall, lanky policeman, owner of the biggest, bushiest eyebrows I have ever seen, handed a folder to the captain and quickly left.

"Well, well. Let's see what we have here. Still nothing to say?"

Shady Dude folded his arms across his chest, sat back in his chair, and smiled.

"Very well, Ernest. We really don't need your input."

Ernest? Vance and I turned to regard the prisoner with a pitiful look. Ernest, having been identified, scowled and, as though someone had flipped a switch, suddenly became *very* cooperative.

"Look, this has just been one huge misunderstanding," Ernest began.

"I don't want to kill you, but I will if I have to," I repeated, as I sat back in my chair and looked at the idiot in handcuffs. "Ring any bells?"

"I was joking, okay?"

"No, you weren't," Vance argued. "You and your pal were caught breaking and entering, on private property."

"You want to help yourself?" Captain Nelson

asked. "You can start by leveling with us. What were you there to do?"

"It's just a misunderstanding," Ernest insisted. Beads of sweat could be seen trickling down the guy's pale forehead. "We were just horsing around."

"We?" Captain Nelson repeated, clearly pleased Ernest had chosen that particular pronoun. "Let's talk about that word. Who were you with?"

Ernest fell silent.

"Come, come, Mr. Beckman. You can do better than that."

Try as I might, I couldn't hold back the snort of laughter. "Beckman? Your name is Ernest Beckman?"

"Yeah? What of it?"

"You tried to intimidate me, threaten to kill me, and your name is Ernest Beckman?"

"Not very scary, is it?" Vance remarked.

"I'll say."

"Talk to me about Stupid," Captain Nelson instructed.

Both Vance and I turned to regard the captain as though he was now speaking tongues.

"What was that, sir?" Vance neutrally asked.

"Stupid," Captain Nelson said. He turned to Ernest and clasped his hands together. Then, resting them on the open folder in front of him, he leaned forward. "It says here that you're a member of something called Stupid. I was giving you a chance to elaborate, because I personally think that has to be the silliest acronym I have ever seen."

"He works for someone with an acronym of S-T-U-P-I-D?" Vance incredulously asked. "That's gotta be a mistake, sir."

"For your information," Ernest hotly snapped, "that's S.T.P.I.D. We're the Strategic Team of Patriotic Irish Descendants."

I held my hands up in a time-out gesture. "Wait. Just wait a minute. You're telling me you work for the forces of STUPID? Is this a joke? Are we being filmed?"

Vance stared at Ernest, waiting for the punch-line he was certain was coming. When nothing more was offered, Vance looked over at the captain and pointed at the police report.

"May I?"

"Of course, Detective."

Now, Captain Nelson might not have been laughing, but I did notice his eyes were watering. The captain must have thought this was the silliest thing he had ever heard, too.

"Ernest Beckman," Vance read, as he skimmed the contents of the police report. "Occupation: custodian. It says here you're a janitor at an elementary school."

"So?" Ernest sneered. "What of it?"

I tapped the open folder. "Where? Here, in PV?"

Vance read a bit farther. "No. Looks like he's from Sacramento, California. Actually, it looks like a suburb just north of Sacramento called Lincoln."

"That's about four hours away," I recalled.

"What do the forces of STUPID do?" Vance idly asked. "Do you guys have a mission statement? Maybe a motto?"

"There is no *U*," Ernest haughtily informed us. "And mock us all you want. It's not like we haven't heard it before."

"What is it you do?" Vance said, as he struggled to keep the smile from forming on his face.

"Whatever we are called to do," Ernest answered. His nose lifted. "Unlike you, we have a cause, and it's one worth fighting for."

"You know what's in the chest, don't you?" I asked.

All eyes turned to me. Ernest stared at me, dumbfounded.

"You couldn't possibly know what the chest contains. It's a secret."

"Not a very good secret," Vance said. "Seriously? Do you really think that silver chest contains the stolen Irish Crown Jewels?"

"I know it does," Ernest insisted. "I just don't know how *you* managed to intercept it."

"Intercept it?" I repeated, confused. "Look, pal, that thing showed up on *my* doorstep. It was addressed to me, and it now falls under my protection. As you might have guessed, I've since moved the chest to a more secure location."

"Where is it?" Ernest demanded. "It doesn't belong to you. It belongs with its rightful owners."

"You're right," I admitted. "I know that thing

doesn't belong to me. If those jewels are, indeed, inside that chest, then I have no problem telling you that I intend to see to it that the jewels are returned to Ireland."

"See?" Vance said, as he looked up at Ernest. "We can all be friends here. We want what you want. We're going to get those things returned to Ireland. You're welcome."

"You can't!" Ernest protested.

"What's that?" Vance asked.

"What was that?" Captain Nelson said.

"Say what?" I added, all at the same time.

"Ireland has no business in owning those famous pieces of history."

"Umm, they're called the Irish Crown Jewels for a reason," I pointed out.

"They belong to the Irish Royal Family," Vance added. "Of course, they're going to get them back."

"There is no Irish Royal Family," I whispered to my detective friend.

"Huh? Sure there is. If there are crown jewels, does that not indicate there's a king and queen?"

"There *was* a king and queen," I said, "later known as the king and queen of England. This was after 1949, when Ireland left the British Commonwealth and was declared a republic."

Vance threw up his hands with frustration. "Okay, Mr. PBS, how do you know so much about this? Oh, let me guess. You wrote a book about Ireland."

I leveled a gaze at my friend. "I've written a lot

of books, buddy, and yes, I've written one about Ireland. Quite recently, as a matter of fact. Ring any bells?"

Vance's eyes widened with surprise. "Oh. Uh, sorry. Forgot about that one."

"You forgot about which one?" Captain Nelson asked.

"Oh, it's nothing, sir. Now, back to you, Mr. Beckman. You claim Ireland has no business owning those jewels? What do you propose to do with them?"

"Maybe he wants to send them to the Queen of England?" I suggested. "After all, at the time of the theft, Ireland fell under England's rule."

"I think he wants them for himself," Captain Nelson said.

"Or else someone in the STUPID organization does," I said. Yeah, I know what you're thinking. I shouldn't keep trying to provoke the guy. Apparently, I have more of an evil streak than I let on.

"Of course we don't want them," Ernest said. "Listen, the Irish Crown Jewels were never associated with any monarchy."

Vance looked at me. "Did you know that?"

"I did, but to be fair, I only learned that about a day or two ago."

"What does that mean for us?" Captain Nelson inquired.

The three of us looked back at Ernest.

"Well, Mr. Beckman?" Vance prompted.

"To give those jewels back would certainly

result in those priceless, historical pieces being broken up and inevitably turned into something else. No, the pieces must remain as they are."

"So, you don't want to give them back," Captain Nelson said, as he tapped his fingers on the table. "What are your plans? What do you plan on doing with them?"

Ernest fell silent.

"Did your STUPID compatriots tell you what their plans are?"

"S.T.P.I.D.," Ernest repeated, through gritted teeth. "They're not stupid."

"Prove it," Vance challenged. "You have yet to tell us what your organization plans on doing with these jewels, provided you ever get your hands on them. Trust me, from the sounds of things, you won't. But, you've piqued our curiosity. Do tell."

Once more, Ernest fell silent.

"Look, Mr. Beckman," Captain Nelson began, using an uncharacteristically sympathetic tone, "say what you will about your ... organization, but everyone at this table can tell that you guys are nothing but amateurs."

"Are not," Ernest sulked.

"You were caught," Vance pointed out.

"So, I was hit with a bit of bad luck. It could happen to anyone."

"You're sitting on that side of the table," Captain Nelson argued, "with a broken leg. You didn't get hit with bad luck. You were knocked out by

Mr. Anderson's wine barrels. A professional would never have allowed himself to be backed into a corner."

"They would have scoped the place out first," Vance added, drawing a nod of approval from the captain. "They would have learned where all the exits could be found."

"There was just the one," Ernest grumped. "What was I supposed to do, make my own door?"

"There are loading docks on three sides of the building," I pointed out. "And two of the walls, the north and the west, have dual loading bays. You didn't even bother to check. If you had, then we most certainly wouldn't be having this conversation."

"We might be able to help you," Captain Nelson said, adopting his soothing tone once more. "We can't do that, though, until you level with us. Tell us more about STUPID."

"S.T.P.I.D.," Ernest insisted.

The captain waived off the correction. "My apologies. Tell us about them."

"We're trying to clear Vicars' name."

The three of us sat forward. This was new. Ernest was finally starting to cooperate! So, the question was, who was Vicars? And why did that name sound familiar?

"What was that?" the captain politely asked.

"Vicars. He was responsible for its security."

"Where is this Vicars now?" Vance wanted to know, as he began taking notes. "Can we talk to him?"

Ernest threw us a condescending look.

"Sir Arthur Edward Vicars was appointed the Ulster King of Arms in 1893, but was fired from the position in 1908, after the theft of the jewels."

"The original theft, back in Dublin," I said, nodding. "Professor Whyte was correct."

Vance turned to me. "Who?"

"When I first started to research that chest," I explained, "I found myself in the library at Medford College. A student recommended I talk to one of her professors, and it turned out she specialized in British history."

"She told you about this theft?" Captain Nelson asked.

"Yes. It's common knowledge in Great Britain. She's the one who managed to identify the Celtic shamrock."

"What Celtic shamrock?" the captain wanted to know.

I pulled out my cell and brought up the pictures I had taken earlier. Zooming in on the uniquely drawn Irish symbol, I passed my phone to Captain Nelson, who reached inside his jacket to retrieve a pair of reading glasses. I watched him study the picture for a few minutes before swiping to the right, and then the left. The captain hesitated after a picture of the entire chest filled the screen.

"Is this it? Is this what all the fuss is over?"

"That chest," Ernest coldly began, "is a price-

CASE OF THE SHADY SHAMROCK

less artifact. It belongs in a museum."

"It belongs with its rightful owner," I argued, growing angry. "This Vicars person, he was STUPID, too, wasn't he? Let me venture a guess. You STUPID guys were responsible for pulling off this heist, but somehow lost track of the chest's location. Now that it has surfaced, for whatever reason, you guys want it back."

Vance and the captain were both nodding. Ernest, on the other hand, was shaking his head.

"Vicars was *not* a member of STUPID. Wait! I mean S.T.P.I.D.! He wasn't a member. Our organization took it upon ourselves to get the jewels away from him."

"Why?" Captain Nelson asked.

Ernest mumbled something, but it was too low to understand.

"Once more, please," the captain ordered.

Ernest let out a loud sigh, as though he was trying to earn himself some sympathy. It didn't work.

"Sir Arthur Vicars admitted, in personal correspondences to his advisor, he was planning on giving the jewels to his daughter, as a wedding present."

"By what right could this guy give away something that didn't belong to him?" I protested.

I was given an appraising stare. "And now you know why the decision was made to remove the jewels to a more secure location."

"Is that how they were stolen?" Captain Nelson asked, as he turned to me. "Were they taken off of

Vicars' daughter?"

"Not according to what I read," I told the captain. "Vicars didn't take the jewels' security too seriously. I guess he was prone to leaving his keys lying around. Heck, they didn't even know the jewels were missing until later in the day, when someone opened the safe for something completely unrelated."

Captain Nelson turned back to Ernest. "Who was responsible for the theft?"

Ernest shrugged. "Does it matter?"

"I'm sure it does to Ireland," Vance muttered, earning a nod of approval from the captain. "Look, Mr. Beckman, perhaps you could tell us what happened after your ST ... er, your *organization* absconded with the Irish Crown Jewels. Were they stashed somewhere in the country? Were they smuggled out?"

"No clue."

"When did this chest resurface?" Captain Nelson asked.

"Last year," Ernest admitted. "The only thing I know is that the chest was discovered in a trunk in the attic of an abandoned house."

"In Wales?" I asked.

"Yes, in a small village. Betws-y-Coed."

"I have no idea where that's at," I confessed.

"That makes two of us," Vance said.

"Better make that three," Captain Nelson added. Then, he turned and asked the question that has been bugging me for some time. "How did that chest get from Wales to Oregon?"

"We'd like to know that, too," Ernest said. "I was asked to not only recover the chest, but to discreetly inquire how you were able to intercept it. I was only told you had it, and that I was to recover it."

Vance turned to the captain. "It has the makings of a clandestine operation, but it sure doesn't feel like one."

Captain Nelson nodded. "Agreed. It's more like … the Three Stooges meet Spy vs Spy."

Ernest frowned, but refrained from saying anything. After a few moments, his gaze dropped to his clasped hands and it stayed there.

"How did you know I had it?" I asked.

Vance turned to look at me and grinned. "And Zack has the winning question of the day. How *did* you know he had the chest?"

"I received a text. It said I was to come here and look for one Zachary Anderson. This is a small town. He wasn't hard to find."

"Who sent the text?" Vance wanted to know. He slid the banker's box that was on the table close to him and started rifling through it. "Let's see if it's … ah. There it is."

Ernest's cell was produced. Vance unsealed the evidence bag and allowed the phone to drop into his hand. From my position at the table, I watched him browse through the smartphone's apps, until the Message app was selected. It only took a few moments to find the message which instructed our friend Ernest, here, to make the journey from Sacramento. However, there was no caller identification, meaning, the sender must have used a burner phone.

A smirk formed on Ernest's face. "See? Told you so."

Captain Nelson frowned. "I'd wipe that smile off your face. You're not off the hook yet. We've got you for breaking and entering, at the very least. Mr. Anderson? You're sure you don't know anyone in Wales?"

"I've been to the northern part of Wales," I admitted, "but I don't have any friends there. At least, none that I'm aware of."

"That suggests someone got their hands on this thing and made the conscious decision to get it to you," Vance said, as he looked at his captain. "We just don't know why."

Ernest suddenly leaned forward in his chair. "Hang on a second. You're suggesting you didn't intercept the chest? You really don't have any idea how it found its way into your hands?"

"None whatsoever," I confirmed. "Found it on my doorstep. Someone sent it to me."

"Impossible," Ernest whispered.

"Believe it, don't believe it, I don't care," I said, shrugging. "No matter how you want to look at it, the chest is going to be returned to its rightful owner, and that sure as heck isn't you, pal."

Captain Nelson cleared his throat. "Ahem. Do we even know if these jewels are in that chest?"

Vance turned to me with a querulous look on his face. I was forced to hold up my hands in an *I don't know* gesture. A thought occurred, which had me turning back to Ernest.

"Captain Nelson brings up a good point. Have you guys confirmed the jewels you so desperately want are even in that chest?"

"I was to open it and confirm their presence as soon as I recovered the chest," Ernest sadly informed us.

"STUPID has never seen the inside of that chest, have they?" I guessed.

"S.T.P.I.D.," Ernest crossly corrected. "And I don't see how that's pertinent."

"I'd say that confirms these jewels are in there," the captain decided. "Am I correct in thinking there's something about the chest which prevents it from being opened? You guys don't have the key?"

"It's a puzzle box," I said. "Don't worry. If there's a way in there, Jillian and I will figure it out."

"Do me a favor?" Vance said, as he, the captain, and I all rose to our feet.

I glanced at my friend. "Sure. What's up?"

"Let the dogs look at it. I think they'll have a better chance at getting it open."

"Vance?"

"Yeah?"

"Bite me."

## SEVEN

I t's very pretty. Do you think it's solid silver? It sure looks like it's all silver, doesn't it?"

"It's not completely silver," I told Jillian, as I ran my fingers over a few of the many marks and carvings on the chest's surface. "It may very well be silver-plated, but it isn't solid. There's some lead in there."

Jillian nodded. "Oh, that's right. I forgot about that. You tried to get the chest x-rayed, didn't you?"

"I did, and no, they couldn't. Nothing but a big, blank square showed up on the monitor."

"Are you sure we couldn't do this upstairs? It's rather gloomy down here. Plus, this is where you were shot. It's not my favorite place to be."

All right, I should establish some context. Since I know the sanctity of my house has been compromised, and for all I know, there could be more bugs in my home than a house infested with a termite colony, I wanted to find someplace else. There had to be somewhere else we could go to study the chest, a place the forces of STU-PID didn't know about. Jillian had volunteered her house, but as you can imagine, there wasn't a snowball's chance in an Arizona summer that I was going to do that. So, where were we?

We were in one of the many secret hideaways found within the mysterious Highland House. No one besides myself, Jillian, Vance, and a few trusted police officers knew *this* particular room even existed. If you want to know where we presently were, then I'd have to refer you to a previous case, when Jillian first purchased this house.

"Couldn't we go to the basement?" Jillian asked, as she nervously looked around. "I don't like it down here. It's okay, Zachary. I had a very secure lock installed on the basement door. Only Lisa and myself have keys."

Lisa Martinez, manager of Highland House, might look unintimidating, especially if you didn't know her, but properly challenged, Lisa wouldn't back down even if a buzzing rattle-snake was involved. She is intelligent, outspoken, attractive, and fiercely loyal. When Jillian mentioned that only she and Lisa had copies of the key, she was telling me that the key was just as secure as being in a safe.

"Fine. I'm sorry. I should've known you aren't a

fan of this room. Sherlock? Watson? Make sure you grab your bones. We're heading to the basement."

Both corgis, who had been stretched out on a large pet bed I had brought with me, looked up at me with their rawhide bones half-sticking out of their mouths. Sherlock's bone already had the knots on either end chewed off, so his looked like a stogie.

"I'm really not too much of a fan of the basement, either," Jillian said. "The sight of you, with …"

I gently placed a finger on her lips. "It's okay. We just need a safe, quiet place to work on *that*."

Jillian looked at the silver chest I was holding and finally nodded. "You're right. Let's see what we can do. Here, give me the chest. Would you set up one of those tables?"

There were four white folding tables leaning up against the wall. Once all four legs had been extended, I dug around a bit and found a few folding chairs. Properly seated, the chest was placed before us and, together, we leaned forward.

"How do you want to start?" Jillian asked.

I shrugged. "Well, we already know there are a lot of moving parts on this thing. I don't know. Perhaps we should make a list of everything that moves? There might be a pattern in there somewhere. Sherlock? Watson? What do you guys think?"

I was ignored. The bones were clearly more interesting than we were. I waited until each of the dogs looked up at me, and just as quickly, we were dismissed.

"So much for that idea. Fine. We're back to taking notes."

Jillian nodded. "Do you still have your notebook with you?"

I pulled a small, bound notebook from my back pocket and unclipped the pen. "Yep. Would you do the honors?"

"Of course. All right. We already know the circle around the English cross rotates. What else?"

"The shamrock. One of the petals moves."

"Which one?" Jillian wanted to know.

I rotated the chest until I was looking at the shamrock. "It's the petal on the right."

I heard the pen scratching against the paper. "Got it. What else?"

"The thistle," I reported. "The stem of the thistle pushes in, like a button."

"Like a button," Jillian softly repeated.

"Also, next to the thistle," I continued, "there's a small square. It can also be pushed, like a button."

"How do you depress the button?" Jillian wanted to know.

Curious, I jabbed a finger at the square next to the thistle. We both heard a soft click as it locked in the down position. After a few moments, I poked it again. There was another soft click, and just like that, the button popped back up to its normal state.

"A second press resets it," Jillian observed, as she scribbled more notes into the notebook. "Anything else?"

"Probably. Let's take a look. I can't see anything else that moves on the front, on the same side as the shamrock," I reported. The chest was rotated, and I was then looking at the side with the Scottish thistle. "I'm looking at the thistle side. It ... hang on! I have some movement here."

Jillian leaned close. "What do you have?"

I tapped several horses. One was rearing, as if it had been spooked. The other appeared to be grazing.

"There are two horses here. The rearing horse? It moves. Not much, mind you, but it moves."

"How much, and in what direction?" Jillian wanted to know.

"Let's say a quarter of an inch, and the horse moves up and down."

"Quarter inch up. Okay. Is there ..."

"The sun!" I exclaimed. "I was going to rotate this thing to the next side, and my fingers brushed by the sun overlooking the two horses. It moved!"

"By how much?"

"Oh, uh, not much. I'd say a quarter of an inch."

"A quarter of an inch again. Hmmm. What about the circle around the clock? Did I ask you how much it rotated?"

"You didn't. Let me check."

"Quarter of an inch?" Jillian asked, a few moments later.

"You called it."

"I'm sensing a pattern here."

I nodded. "Me, too. Okay, moving on. Let's see. We've got moving parts on all sides, except the bottom, which appears to be flat."

"No markings?"

I lifted the chest to inspect the underside. "None that I can see."

"What about the lid?"

"It doesn't have a lid," I argued.

"It does, we just have to figure out how to open it," Jillian insisted. "Okay, I'll rephrase. What about the top? I can see all kinds of things on the lid. Er, well, where the lid *should* be."

I tipped the chest forward and studied the top. Rolling hills, stone circles, and a snarling lion met my eyes. Was this the lion that Burt had mentioned earlier? Experimentally, I nudged the lion's tail. Sure enough, it moved slightly lower, as though it was swishing its tail back and forth.

"The lion. The tail moves, like this."

"Same amount of movement?" Jillian wanted to know.

"Yes. We're still at a quarter of an inch. For the record, Burt noticed this one first."

Jillian nodded. "That's right, I do remember him mentioning something about a lion. Right, what else have you found?"

I poked and prodded the top of the silver box for another minute or so. However, nothing else wanted to move. As I gently let the chest tip backward, so that it was back on the table, I made the mistake of gripping the blasted thing by the top left corner. Before I knew what was happening, the silver box thunked noisily down, on the table. The two corgis glanced up at me, as though they thought I was making too much noise.

"Don't drop it," Jillian warned. "I wouldn't want to hurt anything in there."

"Sorry. Darn thing felt like it slipped out of my … hey, look at that! The corner moved."

Jillian nodded and added the information to her list. "Same amount? Quarter of an inch?"

"Oh. Let me see. Yep. Quarter of an inch."

"Is that it?"

I felt along the sides of the chest and, satisfied there weren't any other surprises, nodded. "I think so. How many does that give us?"

"Eight, I believe."

"Well, where'd you want to start?"

Jillian was silent as she considered. "I don't see any pattern to this. Shamrock, circle, thistle, and square, just to name a few. Perhaps we have to press, or rotate, them in the correct order?"

"It's worth a shot. Okay, let's start with the corner."

"What made you pick that one?" Jillian asked.

I tapped the top of the chest. "For starters, it's on the lid. Figured it couldn't hurt to try."

Jillian shrugged. "Noted. All right, the corner has been rotated. Which one are you trying next?"

"What is closest?"

"From that corner? Let me see. I think it's the thistle, and then the square."

"All right, I've pressed both of them in. Now what?"

"Hmm. The circle and the shamrock are both about the same distance apart. Let's try the shamrock first. And ... now the circle."

"Did anything happen?"

I shook my head. "If something did, then I missed it. All right, moving on. We still have a couple left." The chest was rotated. "I'm trying the rearing horse next."

"'Kay," Jillian said, as she took notes.

"And finally, I'm going to rotate the sun. Ready? Here we go."

Predictably, nothing happened.

"Did you do it?" Jillian asked.

"Yep."

"Nothing happened."

"Yep. Noticed that, too."

"Now what?"

I was silent as I drummed my fingers on the tabletop. "Try them in a different order?"

"Umm, okay."

"Do you have another suggestion?"

"Zachary, how do we know which position constitutes *up* or *down*? On and off. Some might need to be up, and some might need to be down."

Hoo, boy. I hadn't thought of that. It was at this time that my confidence took a very noticeable hit. Jillian laid a hand over mine.

"I'm sorry. I didn't mean to make things difficult."

"Hey, don't worry about it," I said, waving off her concern. "You aren't the one who made that thing, are you? You're not the one who has a devious sense of humor, are you?"

"Should we try a few more?"

I leaned over the table to look down at Sherlock and Watson. Both, I should point out, were busy chewing on their favorite bones and flat-out *ignoring* us. I can only hope that, if they wanted to alert us to something, then they would do something to get our attention. Their current behavior all but proved, unfortunately, Jillian and I were on the wrong track. Oh, well. It couldn't hurt to try!

"Let's try doing this," I started, as I quickly reset the chest. Jillian's statement came to mind, and I had to concede that what I thought of as the starting position was, more than likely, not the *actual* starting position. Still, I was determined to keep trying. "Let's start with horses, and then the sun. Next, let's rotate the circle, hit the thistle, then the shamrock, and the square. Let's add the lion's tail and, finally, let's end with the corner piece. And, what do we have?"

We both stared at the chest in silence.

"Nothing," Jillian conceded. "Zachary, what would you say we try ... Sherlock? Is everything all right?"

Something was up with Sherlock? Since when?

I had just looked at him, and he was heavily involved with his bone. And Watson? She just dropped her own bone and rose to her feet.

"What's going on, guys?" I asked the dogs.

As one, both dogs suddenly looked straight up, at the ceiling. That's when we heard it. There was a loud commotion coming from upstairs, as though someone was stomping around the floor. Lisa was the only one who knew we were down here. Was she trying to signal us?

"Who do you think is up there?" Jillian quietly whispered.

"I have no clue," I admitted. "Were we expecting a herd of elephants to walk through Highland House?"

"Do you think it could be someone looking for the chest?" Jillian asked.

"How? They don't know we're here."

"And only a small group of people know this room is even down here," Jillian added. "Zachary, I think … I think they're somehow tracking the chest!"

"I'd like to think we would have spotted a tracking device long before now," I said.

"What about the cars? You said you already found one, didn't you? Could they have hidden another bug, one where they know you wouldn't have found it?"

"It's possible, but Vance and I have been having our cars swept for bugs on a daily basis. They've come up clean each time."

"What about mine?" Jillian asked, nervously.

"Well, I do think we should probably start sweeping yours, too," I admitted, "but for now? I think we're good. I picked you up at your place, remember?"

"True. Maybe we're overreacting? Maybe it is something beside that organization?"

"What, STUPID? Who knows?"

"So, if they're not tracking the cars, and they're not tracking us, and they're certainly not tracking the chest, what does that leave us?"

"Woof!"

The two of us looked down at Sherlock. He had abandoned his bone yet again and was now glancing suspiciously around the room. I mean, I know dogs have much better hearing than we do, so does that mean Sherlock can hear someone trying to sneak up on us? Had the little pipsqueak just confirmed a long-standing suspicion, which was the amount of English he understood?

"Is there something wrong, pal?" I quietly asked the corgi. "What's going on? Do you smell something?"

Sherlock then turned to Watson and nudged her, as though he wanted her to abandon her bone, too, and join him in the hunt. Watson promptly rose to her feet and was ready to take a step toward me when Sherlock hurried around the table and placed himself directly in her path. He nudged her again and then looked up at me.

"Awwooooo."

"What kind of howl is that?" I wanted to know.

"It sounded like he was telling you off, didn't it?" Jillian said, as she smiled at the dogs.

"Awwooooo."

"Uh, oh," I chuckled. "He second-syllabled us."

"Is there something wrong with Watson?" Jillian asked, concerned. "He just nudged her again. That would be the third time. Sherlock? Is everything okay?"

Sherlock sniffed Watson's collar, looked up at the two of us, then promptly sat. Curiosity had me leaning forward to scratch both of the dogs behind their ears. Watson turned to look at me, as though she wasn't sure she knew what her packmate was doing, and was begging me to intervene. After a few moments, she began scratching at her neck.

"There's no way you picked up a flea," I observed. "What's the matter, Watson? Can I take a look? I promise you I'll give this back to you, girl."

Watson's collar was unbuckled and, while I studied it up close, Jillian scratched the little female's neck with both hands. Watson, unsurprisingly, melted into a red and white pile of goo. Sherlock came up beside Jillian and nudged an arm aside, as if to indicate that the free scratches should be divided equally among all parties.

"Is there anything wrong with her collar?" Jillian asked.

I shook my head. "Not that I can see. Want to take a look? Your eyes are better than mine. Maybe you can spot something I can't."

"Of course."

"Aren't you two the coolest corgis in the whole, wide world?" I praised, knowing full well I sounded like a dopey idiot.

"Oh! Zachary, look at this!"

I turned in time to see Jillian pull a two-inch long *something* out of Watson's collar. From my vantage point, it looked like a piece of thread. Then again, if I wasn't too much mistaken, the tip of the thread had a tiny red light on it, and it was blinking.

"Oh, you've *got* to be kidding me!" I groaned. "Where did you find that?"

"Right here, tucked in the seam. What is it?"

"That, my dear, is yet another bug. Vance found one earlier in my car, and then found one on his."

"Well, here, you take it," Jillian decided, as she hastily dropped the foreign object into my outstretched hand. "I'd just as soon you got rid of it."

"What I want to know," I began, as I pointed at Watson, "is how did this thing get on her collar? Wait. There's no blinking light here. I think ... I think this may just be a GPS tracker."

Jillian nodded. "Oh, so they can't listen in, but can tell where we are, huh? It doesn't make me feel any better."

"You and me both. The question I have is, how could someone have gotten close enough to put this in place?"

"Watson is very friendly," Jillian observed. "Anyone could have approached her and she would more than likely have allowed them. She's very trusting. Did you notice her with anyone earlier?"

I sighed with exasperation and sat back in my chair. "That's a hard question. Those dogs are recognized everywhere we go. People love them, and they love the attention. The corgis always seem to draw a crowd. The Medford college, the PVPD, prepping for the céilí, and even loading up the dogs outside Vance's house."

"Someone wanted to pet the dogs outside Vance and Tori's place? Did you get a look at who it was?"

"No, not really. It was kinda dark out. And, if memory serves, I got the impression that neither of the dogs liked the guy."

"And you let him touch Watson?" Jillian asked, appalled. "I would not have let him anywhere near my animals with a ten-foot pole."

I held up two fingers. "There were two of them, a man and a woman. The man kept his distance, but the woman was friendly. She's the one who gave Watson a few scratches."

"Near her neck?" Jillian asked.

I thought back to the encounter. "Yeah, I believe it was. Son of a gun. I wouldn't have called that."

"What did she look like?" Jillian asked.

"Honestly? She looked like a harmless old grandmother to me. I never would have pegged her for being stupid."

"You mean the acronym, right?"

"Yeah, yeah. Who would've thought it? Maybe S.T.P.I.D. isn't so stupid after all."

"If they know we're here and we have the chest, then what do we do?" Jillian worriedly asked.

"I think we should check Sherlock's collar," I decided. "Just to be safe. Sherlock? Would you come here for a second?"

Let me pause for a moment here. Have you ever taken a collar off your dog and then seen the look of alarm that passes over their features? Think about it. What's going through the dog's head? Well, it's easy. They think they're about to be given a bath.

That must've been what was going through Sherlock's head. He took one look at the loose collar I was now holding and immediately hid behind Jillian.

"It's okay, pal. We just want to check your collar."

Jillian held out a hand. "Want me to do it?"

"Yes, please. Thanks."

Several minutes later, I snapped the collar back in place, much to the relief of one tri-colored pooch.

"There. See? No bath. You're good. So, no bugs on Sherlock, yet we found one on Watson. I say we put it to good use."

"What do you have in mind?" Jillian wanted to know.

"I need time to be able to stash this thing, only

now, thanks to that bug we found on Watson's collar, I'm getting paranoid. Are they still watching?"

Jillian pointed at the needle-like GPS bug in my hand. "They obviously used that thing to follow us here, so I'd say there's a better than average chance they're keeping an eye on it. They'll probably wait us out. Zachary, how are we going to get these people off our backs?"

"I think I have an idea on how we can lose STU-PID."

"S.T.P.I.D.," Jillian corrected.

"Whatever. What time is it?"

"Almost five p.m."

"Good. Here, would you take Sherlock's leash? I'll go upstairs to see if the coast is clear."

It was. Whoever, or whatever, was here earlier had finally left. Lisa was there, manning the counter, along with another employee I didn't recognize. We emerged from one of the side doors in the main hall and, carrying the duffel which contained the chest, approached the counter.

"Everything go okay?" Lisa cheerily asked.

Jillian nodded. "Yes, actually. We heard a lot of movement up here earlier. Is everything okay?"

Lisa nodded. "The Bad Toupee club? I told them that we didn't have anything open."

Both Jillian and I stared at Lisa for a few moments.

"I assumed they were looking for you," Lisa explained. "They wanted permission to inspect the house, claiming they were members of some architecture club. When I told them no, then the story switched to trying to locate a set of lost keys from when one of their members was here earlier. I asked for dates, so I could verify on the computer, which they couldn't give me. By this time, I could tell they knew I suspected something was up, so they made some excuse and split."

"I know they're still out there, watching," I reported, frowning as I did so.

"You do?" Lisa asked. "How?"

I held up the bug found in Watson's collar. "Because of *this*."

Lisa's eyes widened with alarm. "What's that?"

"It's a tracking bug," Jillian reported.

"Ooooo! This is right out of the movies! How cool!"

"They're following us," I reported. "*Not* cool."

"Oh. I'm sorry, Mr. Anderson. I didn't mean ..."

"Lisa?" I smoothly interrupted, "could I get you to do us a favor?"

Highland House's general manager perked up. "Of course. What can I do for you?"

"You're just about done for the day, aren't you?"

Lisa's eyes flitted over to the large clock on the opposite wall. "In about fifteen minutes. Why?"

Jillian smiled. I could see that she knew what I was going to ask her employee to do and nodded approvingly. I handed the bug to Lisa and gave her a grin.

"Would you care to take the scenic route home? Or, better yet, have Kimmi meet you here and maybe go on a joy ride?"

Lisa stared at the tracking bug a few moments before her face broke out in a grin. She had just taken possession of the tiny device when Jillian suddenly frowned. She placed a hand over mine and shook her head.

"Zachary, that isn't going to work. They know what you look like, right? They know what you drive. They're not going to follow Lisa in her car."

Nodding, I unclipped the key to my Jeep and slid it across the counter.

"She's got a full tank. Interested?"

Lisa quickly pulled out her cell.

"Kimmi! Whatcha doin', girl? Hey, what do you say about going on a road trip? Come on down to Highland House. I'll explain it on the way. Awesome. Love you, K."

Fifteen minutes later, Jillian and I, along with Sherlock and Watson, watched my Jeep drive away. I'd like to be able to say that I saw a black Mercedes appear from the shadows and start following, but I can't. Lisa made a left turn and they were gone.

"Think it'll work?" Jillian asked.

I shrugged. "I'd like to think so, provided they didn't bug Highland House when they were here."

Jillian's smile melted off her face. "Oh. I hadn't considered that."

"Don't worry about it. Come on. We need to arrange for some transportation."

Jillian held up her phone. "I have a better idea.

Let me make a few calls."

Less than an hour later, the four of us were in Carnation Cottage, one of Pomme Valley's ten historic houses, which also doubled as Jillian's home. Also present were our friends Vance and Tori, along with Harry and Julie. The pizza had been dropped off about fifteen minutes ago, and judging by the mostly empty box containing what was left of my Hawaiian pizza, I can only assume I had either polished off an entire large pizza by myself, or someone else had a few slices without me noticing.

I sincerely hoped it was the latter.

"Great idea," I told Jillian, as we took the loveseat in her living room.

Only when the remaining four had claimed seats, and the dogs were snoozing on the rug in front of us, did I unzip the duffel bag on the coffee table and lift out the chest. Vance nudged his wife and inclined his head toward the table.

"Is that it? Is that what this fuss is about?"

"That's it, all right," I confirmed.

"So, it's a silver box," Harry observed. "What's so special about it, man?"

"We had our cars bugged so someone would be able to keep an eye on us," Vance reported, which drew a gasp of surprise from Julie. "There's a group of people in town that really want to get their hands on that thing."

"Do you know who?" Julie asked.

Julie Watt also worked at the police station,

only she wasn't a police officer. Her role was to fill in wherever she was needed. Sometimes, she'd be the one manning the front desk and would, therefore, be the one dealing with the general public. Other times, she'd fill in on the emergency dispatch line.

"The forces of STUPID," I automatically answered.

Vance snorted with amusement, while the other three simply stared at me with confusion written across their features.

"The people who bugged your cars are stupid?" Julie hesitantly asked.

"In this day and age, they would be," Harry decided. "Modern electronics can usually be traced back to a manufacturer, bro, so yeah, I can get on board with them being stupid."

"Not stupid, but STUPID," I clarified. "They're Irish descendants, I guess."

"Irish people are *not* stupid," Tori declared, growing angry.

Jillian held her hands up in a time-out gesture.

"Hang on, Tori. I think we have a miscommunication going on here. Zachary keeps saying stupid, but he really means S.T.P.I.D., don't you, dear? It's an acronym."

"Potato, potahto."

It was Harry's turn to call a time-out.

"Just a moment, bro. The people after you? They're Irish?"

I looked at Vance. "Do you remember what that

silly acronym stood for?"

Vance pulled out his notebook. "Yeah. Just a moment. Okay, here it is: Strategic Team of Patriotic Irish Descendants."

"S-T-P-I-D," Tori observed. She looked at me and laid a hand over mine. "I'm sorry, Zack. I misunderstood."

"Don't sweat it. Jillian is right. I've been calling them stupid for several days now. Whatever. Anyway, this ... group of people bugged my Jeep and Vance's car. They also managed to slip a bug into Watson's collar."

Vance stiffened with surprise. "Seriously?"

"We found it earlier today."

Sherlock lifted his head from the rug and turned to regard me with a piteous expression.

"All right, fine. *He* found it. Satisfied, your Royal Canineship?"

Sherlock let out a soft snort and returned to his nap.

"This is getting spooky," Julie said. "Bugs on your cars are one thing, but trying to bug one of your dogs?"

"How *did* they pull that one off?" Vance wanted to know.

"I think it happened at your house," I began. "There was an older couple outside. The man didn't approach, but the woman stopped to pet Watson."

Tori's eyes widened with shock. "I remember them! I actually said something to Vance about it later that evening. Wasn't it something about having never seen them before?"

"We know everyone around us," Vance explained.

I pointed at the chest. "Well, now that we know people are after Pandora's Box here, Jillian and I are hoping you'll be able to help us figure out how to open this thing up."

"Is it locked?" Harry asked. "How hard can it be? Come on, man, didn't you say you could pick locks now?"

"I'm an amateur," I clarified, "and if that had a keyhole, then I'd certainly give it a try."

"We think it's a puzzle box," Jillian added.

Tori perked up. "Like those Japanese puzzle boxes? Certain panels slide in specific directions, and once all steps have been taken, the box opens?"

Jillian nodded. "Yes, exactly."

"Have you figured out how to get it open yet?" Vance asked. "If all else fails, I have an acetylene torch you can borrow."

"Nuh-uh. We can't risk harming the contents."

"And that would be …?" Harry asked.

"Some mighty pricey valuables," I answered.

"You think there's jewelry in there?" Vance asked.

"We think so," I said. "This might come as a surprise to you guys, but we're pretty sure that the stolen Irish Crown Jewels might be in there."

The room fell silent.

"How mysterious!" Tori exclaimed.

"This is exciting!" Julie echoed.

"That'd be one helluva case to break," Vance added.

"The Irish have crown jewels?" Harry wanted to know.

All of us turned to look at Harry. I'd also like to point out that both dogs roused themselves from their nap to regard Harry with a neutral look.

"What?" Harry stammered, growing defensive. "I thought the crown jewels were a British thing."

"For the record," I said, coming to Harry's aid, "I was right there with you, pal. I didn't know Ireland had crown jewels, either. But, from what I've recently learned, I can tell you that the jewels weren't worn by monarchs. They were more for presentation, I guess."

"Do you really think those missing jewels are in there?" Julie quietly asked.

"That's the running theory," I confirmed.

Harry pointed at the chest. "What made you think *that* has these missing jewels, bro? What do you know that we don't?"

I tapped the side of the chest with the shamrock. "*That* is the answer. This is a very distinctive shamrock. Thanks to a new friend in Medford, I've learned it was last seen in a series of newspaper articles from the 1930s or 1940s."

Vance rubbed his hands together. "Well? Let's get crackin'. I've got twenty bucks that says we'll be able to get this thing open by, what, eight p.m.?"

"It's just after six," I reported, as I checked my cell. "And I say you won't."

Vance tapped the bill he had dropped next to the chest. "Put up or shut up, buddy."

Less than ten minutes later, the amount of cash on the table was more than a hundred dollars. Having already tried my luck with the chest, I remained in my seat, with my arm around Jillian. Together, the two of us watched our friends try to find some combination of movements, in order to open the chest. However, their luck resembled mine. After three solid hours of poking, prodding, twisting, and turning, they were no further along than I was, and that was after I had spent an entire night trying to get the blasted thing to open.

"I think we're going about this wrong," Jillian said, as the chime of her grandfather clock announced it was now after nine p.m.

"What do you mean by that?" I wanted to know.

Jillian pointed at the chest. "If we're to go under the assumption that this box is, in fact, a puzzle box, then I think we're trying to solve this thing incorrectly."

"We're listening," Vance said.

"Himitsu-Bako," Jillian began. "Who among us have ever tried to open a traditional Japanese secret box?"

A quick check of the table confirmed no one had ever touched one.

"All right," Jillian continued, "I thought as much. You have to understand how most of those puzzle boxes worked. First, you find a piece that moves. Not by much, of course, but just enough."

"Just enough to *what*?" Tori asked.

"Just enough to allow the second piece to move," Jillian answered.

As one, we all turned to regard the chest. I leaned forward to tap the shamrock.

"All right, so, this shamrock, for example. This leaf moves. So, if I was to move it like this, then … I would need to look for another part to move? That's easy. There are several other pieces that'll move."

"What about pieces that don't?" Julie asked.

"Pieces that don't?" I repeated. "What does that mean?"

A look of surprise appeared on Tori's face. A few moments later, that same look moved over to Julie.

"Oh!" Harry's wife exclaimed. She looked at Tori, and then Jillian. "I get it. Now, *that* makes sense."

I glanced over at Harry, and then Vance, who shrugged.

"Care to share? What'd we miss?"

"Himitsu-Bako will open with steps," Jillian explained. "You have to find the first step. Once that piece moves, then you have to look for something that previously didn't move, and then …"

"… try to move it," I breathed, amazed. "If it

moves, then that's step two. How many steps will there be?"

Jillian shrugged. "The box I have, which I still need to bring over here so you can see for yourself what I mean, is eleven steps. This chest could be less, and just as easily, it could be more."

"Swell," I muttered. "How does that help us here? There are, what, seven or eight pieces that already move?"

"Then, that means there are seven or eight possible first steps," Jillian reported. "One of them must be the right one."

I looked at the other members of our group and smiled. "All those in favor of allowing Jillian to try her luck on the chest?"

The five of us simultaneously raised our arms. Jillian blew me a kiss and promptly shooed me off the loveseat.

"While she's doing that," Vance said, "I'm gonna go out to the car. I've got something for you."

"You do? Well, color me intrigued. Any ideas?" I asked Tori, after Vance had walked out the front door.

"Not a clue."

A few moments later, Vance was back, and he was holding what looked like a thick, black wand.

"What's that?" I asked.

"It's an RF wireless signal detector wand. It runs off a single AA battery. This baby will detect all radio transmitters, from 50MHz to 6GHz."

"And I can borrow it?" I hopefully asked.

"For a day or so. I've got a buddy in Medford who is a serious conspiracy theory fanatic. He thinks the government is out to get him, so he's a little on the paranoid side."

I edged closer, noted the make and manufacturer of the wand, and quickly looked them up online. Sure enough, they were listed on Amazon's website. Granted, they were pricey, but not nearly as much as I had expected.

I ordered two.

"Show me how it works," I instructed.

For the next ten minutes, we all watched Vance walk around the room and check for bugs. Thankfully, nothing was found. We went out to our cars and watched as Vance gently waved the wand an inch or two above the surface of each car.

They were clean, too.

Once we were certain the forces of STUPID, er S.T.P.I.D., hadn't bugged any of our cars, or Jillian's home, we each breathed a sigh of relief.

"What does this tell us, bro?" Harry asked.

I shrugged. "I'm not sure. I thought for sure that we'd have found another bug or two by now. Perhaps our STUPID pals are on a limited budget and couldn't afford more than two or three bugs? Who can say?"

In less than twelve hours, I would be able to answer that, only the answer I'd give wouldn't be what anyone would want to hear.

# EIGHT

W e haven't done this in a while, have we? Granted, the last time we were in this thing, we kinda found a dead person, so all I ask is that you two keep your noses in the cab, all right?"

As expected, both corgis ignored me. They were too busy creating what every dog owner on the planet was familiar with, namely, numerous streaks on windows affectionately labeled nose art. In this case, we were in the cab of the winery's John Deere tractor, and were headed back to the north fields. Yes, that was where the remains of a certain someone had been found, but this time, thankfully, I wasn't going to use my tractor to break up any rocks. There was a large, dead tree near the northwestern border of the property, and I was determined to get rid of that eyesore once and for all. The problem was, it was about a fifteen minute drive for me to get this beast all the way out there.

If you haven't guessed it by now, it was the following day. Jillian still had possession of the chest, and she assured me she had the perfect hiding place for it. In case the Forces of STUPID, as I've started calling them in my head, had somehow managed to bug our phones, I forbade Jillian from mentioning its location. The less I knew, the better.

So, discovering I had some free time on my hands, since my latest book was in the hands of my editor, and I hadn't decided which of my dozen or so writing projects would be next, I decided to make myself useful. I could claim that I meant to say, something useful for the winery, but let's face it. Everyone who knows me will know how much I love playing with the biggest toy I own. Therefore, it didn't take very long for me to snatch the keys off the peg in the winery and head for my tractor. All in all, it took a solid twenty minutes of driving to make it from the storage shed all the way out to the extreme northwestern corner of my property.

"You two stay here," I ordered, as I grabbed my gloves and a set of chains I kept under the buddy seat. "We're going to rip this sucker apart. What do you say?"

I was ignored again. You'd think I would be used to it by now.

Two hours later, there was nothing left of Ol'

Nasty—a term of endearment by yours truly—but a jagged, scarred stump. Deciding the tractor probably wasn't strong enough to rip the blasted thing out of the ground using nothing but the chains, I set to work clearing and breaking as many roots as I could find. Also, since I couldn't very well dig down to expose the northern roots of the tree without ripping into the road itself, I had to settle on digging as much as I could from the southern side, all without destabilizing the hillside. I'd like to say I was just being cautious, but thanks to the infamous power pole incident from earlier this year, I've learned to be a little more observant of the surrounding area.

I know you'd like me to elaborate on that, but since it's still a sore subject, and one that cost me a pretty penny to straighten out, all I'll tell you is never dig too close to a utility pole. If the stupid thing starts to lean in any direction, then the utility company *will* be right out to fix it *and* give you the bill. Turns out, the power company really doesn't like it when people tinker with their sacred poles. It's been three months since *The Incident* and I don't think the power company has forgiven me. Whatever.

Keeping an eye on the nearby road, I started working the controls. Push that in there, lift that lever there, and push on that pedal down there. It may seem monotonous to you, but I challenge you to get behind the seat of one of these things and not have a huge smile plastered on your face. This piece of machinery radiated power, and I couldn't be happier to apply that power to something I've been eyeing ever since I realized it was on my land.

The roots were broken, and the stump was now leaning precariously to the right, *away* from the road. Sensing Ol' Nasty was about to give up the ghost, I started grinning like an idiot. Securing chains around the stump, and then fastening them to the bucket, I gave the corgis a good-luck scratching.

"Here we go, guys. Can we all say, dump the stump?"

There must've been a root or two that I missed, because Ol' Nasty refused to budge. Cursing, I dropped the gear into first and eased the tractor backward. We played tug-of-war for a minute or two before the first crack sounded, which caused the three of us to jump in our seats. Sherlock and Watson both started woofing and checking all directions, as though they both thought we were about to be attacked by a wave of zombies.

"We're good guys. It's just the stump. I think that means we won this round. Hopefully, there won't be another."

My cell rang, proving just how often I'm wrong.

"Hey, Vance. What's up?"

"Zack, where are you?"

"In the tractor, working on removing…"

"Forget about that for now," Vance interrupted. "Where's the chest?"

"Honestly? I don't know, pal. Jillian said …"

"*Not over the phone!*" Vance hissed.

Something was up. Why did it sound like Vance was on edge?

"What's the matter, pal? Is something wrong?"

"The S.T.P... You know what? I'm tired of calling him that. The stupid guy! He's escaped!"

All right. That caught my attention. The bucket was lowered, I inched the tractor forward to relieve the tension on the chain, and brought my favorite toy down to an idle.

"Say that again, please?"

"The guy escaped!"

"Are you kidding me?" I demanded. "How is that even possible in this day and age? They don't have prison breaks, do they? Did you guys lose everyone or just him?"

"Just him!" Vance all but shouted. "And he didn't escape from our jail but from the hospital. He has a broken leg, remember? Well, he complained his leg was bothering him, so while he was being checked by the doctor, he somehow managed to make it out of the hospital, unobserved."

"With a broken leg?" I sputtered.

"I know, right?"

Right about then, I realized why Vance was calling. If these people had the ability to sneak their members away from a guarded hospital room, then that meant they were more of a threat than we had given them credit for, and that meant it was time to track down Jillian.

"I'm on it, pal. Hold up, I'll call you back. Sherlock? Watson? Come on. We're bailing out."

The three of us sprinted from the tractor and approached the road. There, coming toward me, was a 2015 Volkswagen Beetle, and it was pink. I knew of only one person who drove a car like that, and she just so happened to spend a lot of time at the winery.

It was Kim, one of Lentari Cellars' interns. I watched her eyes widen with surprise as soon as she saw me, and she immediately brought her car to a stop. Rolling down her window, she leaned out.

"Mr. Anderson? Are you okay?"

"I'm good, Kim, thanks. Hey, could you give us a lift back to the winery? If I try to drive that beast back, then it'll be a good twenty to twenty-five minutes before we make it home."

"Sure, hop in. Are you sure everything's all right?"

"Sherlock? Watson? Back seat. Move. Umm, I'm not sure. I don't want to take any chances. So, if you would, could you floor it?"

This particular Beetle only had about 150 horsepower, but it was more than adequate to get us back to the winery in under five minutes. Thanking the girl profusely, I gathered up the dogs and sprinted for my Jeep. Careful not to touch the caked-on mud that was *everywhere*, I got the door open and the dogs settled in the back seat.

In case you were wondering, Lisa and Kimmi had an absolute field day with my Jeep yesterday. Having never driven an off-road vehicle, they ended up taking several back roads out of town and then explored much of the countryside, all without the help of any road.

In fact, they enjoyed the off-roading experience so much that, once Lisa returned the keys to me last night, she insisted they were going to trade one of their cars in for a Jeep. Now, however, my Jeep was caked with mud. Lisa offered to pay for it to be cleaned, but I assured her it really wasn't necessary. Whether or not the Forces of STUPID fell for the bait, and followed Lisa out of town, I didn't know. I'd like to think we wasted their time, but until we could talk to one of them, I didn't think we'd ever know. I made a mental note to take it through a car wash at the next opportunity, but for now, there were more pressing matters at hand. Once I finally made it to the road, I decided to call Jillian.

"Zachary! What a pleasant surprise! What…?"

"Are you okay?" I interrupted. "Tell me you're all right."

"I'm all right," Jillian assured me. "What's the matter? Why would you ask that?"

"The guy we caught breaking and entering at the winery? He escaped."

"From jail? How is that possible?"

"Not from jail, but from the hospital. Long story short, he's on the loose, and I think he must have had help. So, the, uh, milkshake. Is it safe? I really don't want anything to happen to it."

"The milkshake," Jillian slowly repeated.

Spontaneous code-name designations aren't really my strong suit. Hopefully, my fiancée knew me well enough to be able to figure out what I was trying *not* to say.

"It's fine, Zachary. It's ..."

"There's no need to tell me now," I hastily interrupted. "As long as it's secure and you're safe. That's all I care about. Where are you now?"

"I'm at my store."

"Perfect. I'll be there in about fifteen minutes."

I wasn't even close. Five miles from town, I hit the one thing that Pomme Valley was *not* known for: traffic. What was going on? Was there an accident ahead? Fire? Plague? Locusts?

Thirty minutes later, as I finally made it to downtown PV, I discovered the answer. This was the first day of a wine festival, where each of the twenty-four wineries which called PV home could compete among themselves to see who was favored by the townsfolk. Think of it as a People's Choice Award, given by the good citizens of Pomme Valley to reward their favorite wine. And, not to toot my own horn, but every time Lentari Cellars has entered, we won, hands down. I knew Caden was planning on entering again, but whether or not he had already set up the winery's booth, I didn't know.

So, why would that mean so many people would flock to PV? It's easy. Free wine. Yes, you heard that right. In an effort to attract more customers, the local wineries were encouraged to give away free samples of their wares. Let me tell you, *nothing* will attract a crowd more than free drinks.

"Swell," I grumbled, as I navigated my way through the bumper-to-bumper traffic.

Just as I had surmised, there was no parking to be found anywhere. However, I had an ace up my sleeve. There was a small alley that ran between Main and C Street, and next to the dumpster allotted for Cookbook Nook's use was just enough room to park a couple of vehicles. It was where Jillian typically parked when she was there. Granted, her employees could be parked back there, too, and there might not be any room left, but at least it was worth a try.

"And ... we're in luck, guys. Look, there next to Jillian's car? I can fit the Jeep there."

Gathering up the dogs' leashes, we approached the back door. Before I could fire off a text message, the door opened and I was looking at Cassie's smiling face. The high school teenager grinned at me and held the door open.

"Ms. Cooper suspected you might try to park back here."

"She suspecteth correctly, milady," I drawled, which elicited a giggle from Jillian's employee. "The parking doth sucketh rocks out yonder."

Cassie laughed again. "Well, come on in. Ms. Cooper is currently dealing with an irate customer."

"Irate? How irate?"

"One of the espresso machines had been moved to a different spot on the shelves. The person who brought it to her attention is insisting she honor the price that was below it, even though the price tag clearly shows it isn't for the same product."

I followed the girl through Cookbook Nook's backroom as we headed to the main floor.

"How much of a price difference is it?"

"Less than half."

"I hope she doesn't cave."

Cassie turned to look at me. "Trust me, she won't."

"Have you guys been busy?"

The teenager paused at the staff door to look back at me. "Like you wouldn't believe. It's crazy. I mean, it's a good-crazy, but wow, do these festivals bring out the kooks."

"Don't I know it," I grinned, as I followed her out, into the store.

Crazy was an understatement. It was standing room only. No matter where I looked, all I could see was a veritable sea of faces. I worriedly looked down at the dogs. I couldn't navigate through *that*, could I? What if Sherlock and Watson were hurt? What if someone accidentally stepped on them?

The guesswork was taken out of my hands. Sherlock's ears jumped straight up. His nose lifted and I could see that he was sniffing the air, as though he had caught a whiff of something tantalizing. Watson looked up at me, her stump of a tail wiggled, and then she looked straight ahead, at the crowds of people milling about.

"Woof."

I looked back at Sherlock. He was now looking at the crowds of people, too, and just like that, I felt a tug on their leashes.

"Don't even think about it," I cautioned. "Do you have any idea what the odds are that someone would step on you out there? It's wall-to-wall people. There's no way I'm going to let two small …"

Sherlock and Watson surged forward, which had the effect of yanking me off balance. Just like that, I had to start apologizing.

"Pardon me. I didn't mean to … I'm so sorry. It's the dogs, really. Do you see them down there? No, I guess you wouldn't. They're already off. I'm so sorry, ma'am. Yes, I know the dogs just went through your legs. I'm not sure how to … all right, that works. Sherlock? Would you stop? I … hey there, Mayor Campbell. How are you? Huh? Why is there a leash wrapped around your legs? Sherlock and Watson are down there somewhere, and they're trying their hardest to get me in trouble, I swear."

Several dozen apologies later, we made it to the front of the store. There was a steady stream of people entering, but I didn't see anyone leaving. No wonder there was hardly any room to breathe.

I felt the leashes go taut once more. Sherlock and Watson still weren't visible, but I did see a line of people suddenly look down, which made me think the corgis had to be up there, somewhere.

"Here we go again. Hi! Terribly sorry. Don't mind me. Dog owner coming through. You know how it is, ma'am, don't you? No? Just me? Of course. Pardon me, coming through."

Now I could see what was happening. Jillian had wisely opened up her store's second door. Cookbook Nook had long ago expanded to the shop next door, which meant that particular door was usually locked and would display a sign on the door that instructed customers to use the other door. Well, on this particular day, Jillian had put a big *Exit* sign on the door and had it propped open, outside. The dogs were angling straight for the exit.

What was going on? Who were the dogs following? And where was Jillian? I really needed to let her know I was here.

I made it outside and, once I had the corgis in sight, took up the slack in the leashes. Irritated, both dogs turned to look back at me, as though I had no business asking them to slow down. Sherlock woofed once and headed left, toward the east.

"What the blazes are you after?"

My phone began ringing. One look at the display showed that it was Jillian. "Hey, are you okay? I'm sorry. I got pulled out of..."

"Zachary!" Jillian all but shouted into the phone. It also sounded as though she was near tears. "I'm so sorry! I don't know how it happened!"

"What's the matter?" I worriedly asked.

I gave a quick tug on the leash, indicating we were stopping. However, the dogs wouldn't have any of it. I was forcefully pulled along the sidewalk, amidst the crowd of festival-goers. Yes, I was stronger than the dogs, and could have physically pulled them to a stop. However, there was something about their behavior that had me continuing to walk forward.

"It's gone, Zachary!" Jillian sobbed. "The ch—… milkshake! It's gone!"

"It was at the store?" I asked, more surprised than angry.

"It was in my backroom. I had it sitting in a toaster box, stacked with the rest of my inventory. I thought it would be a good hiding place. I don't understand! No one knew it was there!"

"Someone must've planted a bug somewhere near you," I theorized. "That's the only way they could've known."

"Where are you?" Jillian asked. "Cassie told me that she let you in the back door, but I don't see you anywhere."

"The dogs pulled me out the door. Of course! That must be what they're after! Somehow, Sherlock and Watson zeroed in on someone who aroused their suspicion. That particular someone, whoever it is, has left the store. That must be why I was pulled outside!"

"You're telling me you're following the person responsible for stealing the … milkshake?"

"There's no need to use the milkshake moniker anymore. They have it. We have to get it back."

"I'm calling Vance," Jillian decided.

"Good. Tell him I'm currently on Main Street, heading east."

"I'm on it, Zachary. Stay safe. I don't want you confronting anyone, is that understood?"

"Hey, I'm only …"

"Promise me," Jillian insisted.

"Fine. I won't put myself in any danger."

"Good. Keep your phone close."

"Always do, my dear."

We continued east on Main Street for the next ten minutes. Yes, you read that right. This had to be the slowest chase I think I have ever participated in. Either the dogs were chasing someone who was down on all fours and *crawling* over the ground, or else we were following someone who was unconcerned about being caught. I just wish I could tell who we were chasing. There were still too many people on the sidewalk with me to determine who we were after.

My cell rang again. This time, it was Vance. Putting the call on speakerphone, I held it out in front of me as I continued to let the dogs lead the way.

"Vance?"

"Where're you at, buddy? Jillian just told me the, um, er, *it* was stolen. Are you really following the thief?"

"I think so. I'm letting Sherlock and Watson do the leading. Thus far, we've made it less than two blocks. We're still on Main Street, about halfway between 4th and 5th Street."

"I know where you're at. And you really don't know who you're chasing?"

"The only thing I can tell you is that we are going really slow. There are still tons of people everywhere, so I don't have a description for you. Sorry. I'm hoping that ... hold on, Vance. Sherlock? Watson? Look, guys. It may be easy for you two to navigate through this many people, but for me? A little more difficult. I'm tired of apologizing to people. Let's show a little ... I'm so sorry, ma'am. I had no idea my dogs were going to do that. Here, let me lower the leashes, and you can step over. I'm so sorry. You, er, have yourself a good day. Sherlock? Do that again, you little booger, and you're gonna lose your treat privileges tonight, is that understood?"

An empty threat, to be sure. When it came to Sherlock and Watson's comfort, I have been known to sacrifice my own needs so those two could have a better life. What did that actually translate to? Me, refusing to budge, when both dogs were draped across my lap and I had long ago lost feeling in both legs.

Dogs.

"Vance? I'll call you back."

After the blonde woman had carefully stepped over the leash, and given me a rather stern look,

I decided it was time to figure out who we were chasing. Pulling the corgis to a stop, and stepping out of the line of traffic, I discovered we were presently in front of 4th Street Gallery, Zora Lumen's business. Those familiar with my history will know how much I don't care for this particular store, and thankfully, I didn't have to go inside. In fact, I could see Ms. Lumen herself, looking just as gaunt as I remembered, and dressed exactly how I would expect Gomez Addams to look if encountered in real life. She was tending to something at her desk, but just as soon as I mentally implored her to keep her head down, she naturally looked up at that time and locked eyes with me.

Right-o. It was time to move on. Wrapping the leashes tightly around my hand, we moved off. I halfway expected the corgis to pull like crazy, since by this time, our adversary should have gained a considerable advantage. However, based on how slowly the dogs were moving, either we were following a group of snails, or else this person wasn't trying to flee at all.

Who in their right mind, I thought angrily, would choose to flee at such a slow speed? They clearly managed to locate and steal the one thing everyone seemed to want. They had to know they would be pursued, and yet, here we were, going no faster than the group of seniors who had been allowed to venture outside for the first time in years!

Seniors? Seniors were slow. Seniors couldn't

move that fast. And, thinking back to the encounter outside Vance's house, wasn't that couple on the older side, too? They were easily in their seventies.

We increased our pace until we were less than a dozen feet away from the front of the herd, so to speak. And, out front, dictating what pace the rest of us would be taking, were four seniors shuffling harmlessly along. Well, let me amend that by specifying two were using canes and the other two were in small, motorized carts. They were chatting, laughing, and pointing at various things as they passed by.

Frowning, I looked at the dogs and shook my head.

"This can't be right, guys. Look at them. They look harmless. Are you sure?"

The dogs only had eyes for the group of seniors. In fact, I could narrow that down and say they only had eyes for the two people driving the little scooters. And, as I slowly walked back and forth across the sidewalk, weaving from the left to the right, we were able to triangulate even further. The little old lady with the white frizzy hair, driving the scooter closest to us, had captured the dogs' attention. So, while the seniors chatted frivolously away, I was able to hang back and study the cart.

This scooter had a small basket up front, below the handlebars, and a larger, flat cargo area behind the seat. Since there were only a few small shopping bags in the basket, I concentrated on the cargo area. There was a cardboard box there, loosely covered by a shawl, bungee-corded in place. Plus, I do seem to recall Jillian saying that she had hidden the chest in a toaster box. So, the question was, is the box on the back of that scooter a toaster's box?

We made it to the intersection of Main and 5$^{th}$ Street. While we waited for the opportunity to safely cross the street, I fired off a text to Vance, to let him know I'm pretty sure I identified the suspects: seniors. And, what's more, I was certain a little old lady had the chest strapped to the back of her scooter. Vance's response?

SERIOUSLY?

It may have been a text message, but I could easily hear the skepticism in that response. I snapped a photo and sent it to him, just so he could see what I was looking at. About to argue my point, one of the men in the group suddenly pointed across the street at Bartlett House, which was one of PV's ten historic houses. Presumably, they wanted to take a closer look. The group of four broke off from the rest of the crowd and patiently waited to cross Main Street. I was able to duck behind a large family while we waited.

Of course, my phone decided that now would be a good time to chirp like a cricket, which signified I had an incoming text message. However, I was too close to the seniors to respond. With the traffic on Main coming to a halt, our group headed off, across the street. While the seniors chatted among themselves, and consulted some tourist pamphlets, I stepped off to the side and texted Vance.

AM SURE THEY'RE INVOLVED. CURRENTLY IN FRONT OF BARTLETT HOUSE.

A stiff breeze appeared, and promptly blew up a corner of the shawl-covered box. A picture of a shiny toaster was revealed. Surprising myself, and not really sure how I wasn't in control of my own body, I stepped forward, hastily unhooked the bungee cords, and reclaimed the box. Tucking the 'toaster' securely under my arm, I took a few steps back.

Two of the seniors, the ones who were not driving little scooters, turned to look at me with the sheerest look of disbelief on their face. I held up the box and gave them a little bow.

"I do appreciate you guys watching this thing for me. I'd hate to think what would happen if it were to fall into the wrong hands, don't you?"

"What do you think you're doing, young man?" an elderly woman exclaimed, throwing a decent amount of outrage into her voice.

The owner of the scooter, who had been carrying the box, executed a perfect 180-degree turn in her little vehicle and was now facing me. The moment I locked eyes with the woman, they widened with surprise. It was the same lady who had greeted Watson outside Vance's home, only she was now wearing a frumpy yellow sun dress and a white wide-brimmed hat. She was also wearing a frizzy white wig under that hat.

"Nice hair," I told the woman. "If you haven't already figured it out, we found the bug you planted on Watson's collar. Hey, does anyone else hear that? Is someone's cell ringing? Oh, wait. My bad. I think that's me."

Pretending I was receiving a call, I pulled out my phone and quickly snapped pictures of the speechless group. Then, right before my eyes, the seniors scattered. Canes were discarded, as were the two scooters. They each took a separate direction and, before I even knew what was happening, they disappeared. I'd also like to point out that those seniors moved as though they were thirty years younger than they appeared. Then again, that could very well be the case.

I heard a wailing siren approach. Granted, it couldn't move that fast, since the traffic was nearly bumper to bumper, but at least the cars *tried* to move out of the way. I watched my friend's Oldsmobile sedan pass us, heading westbound, on Main Street. Vance locked eyes with me from across the street, executed an immediate U-turn, and pulled up alongside me. He was out of the car even before it came to a stop.

"Where are they, Zack? Tell me you know where they ... that box. It's about the right size for ... tell me it's ..."

"You really ought to start finishing your sentences, pal," I laughed. "I haven't checked yet, but I think we're both going to be pleasantly pleased with what is in here."

"Did you get a look at who did this? And what's this? They left their scooters behind?"

I pointed at a label on the back of the scooter, near one of the brake lights.

"It's rented."

Vance retrieved one of the two canes currently leaning up against the white picket fence surrounding Bartlett House.

"And these? I can't imagine someone who needed a cane to walk around would willingly leave them here."

"They didn't need them," I clarified. "Cane or scooter. As soon as I snagged the box off the back of that scooter there, the driver of this one turned around. Vance, it was the same lady who had placed that bug on Watson's collar."

"The very same?"

"She was wearing a white wig this time, but yeah."

"I just wish you could have gotten their pictures."

I held up my phone and waggled it. "I did. That was when they scattered, and I do mean *scattered*. The two using canes abandoned them and took off, as did the two drivers of the scooters. The four of them headed off in different directions."

Vance pointed at the box. "Let's see if our luck

will hold. Care to do the honors?"

"Absolutely," I said, as I dropped the shawl that had been covering the box onto the storage rack on the scooter.

The box was opened and the two of us peered inside. There, looking just how I remembered seeing it, was the silver chest with the shamrock symbol.

# NINE

"T his has got to be the stupidest case I've ever worked," Vance said, ten minutes later. After realizing how that sounded, my detective friend gave us a sheepish smile and shrugged. "I guess it fits with their name, doesn't it?"

"The Forces of STUPID," I said, agreeing.

"I've never heard of seniors behaving this way," Jillian added.

We were currently in one of the Pomme Valley police station's two conference rooms. Vance, seated at the head of the rectangular table, stared at the silver chest in front of me and shook his head. I sat back in my own chair, leaned down to ruffle the fur on both Sherlock and Watson's heads, and looked over at Jillian.

"You had the chest in the backroom, didn't you? Where at? And how could they have snuck in there to take it?"

Jillian nodded. "I wish I knew, Zachary. There's plenty of stock back there. Cassie had just unboxed a toaster, to replace one that had recently sold, and was preparing to flatten the box. I decided it would make a good hiding place, so after stowing the chest—or milkshake, you silly man—inside the box, I sealed it up and placed it among the ten others that were there."

"Yet, someone knew you had it," Vance observed.

Jillian shrugged. "That's the only thing I can think of. It makes me angry. That means someone has placed a bug in my store. I need to purchase one of those bug-wand devices for my own personal use."

"You'll have yours by tonight," I told her, as I placed my hand over hers. "I ordered two the day Vance brought that thing over and scanned the house. There's one for me, and one for you."

"How sweet! Thank you, Zachary."

"Those aren't cheap, pal," Vance said.

"I know. However, there are some things that are worth it. This is one of them."

"Senior citizens planting bugs," Vance scoffed. "The Forces of STUPID were using canes and scooters. What's next? Hiding the chest in a case of prune juice?"

"Personally, I think it's the perfect disguise," Jillian said. "They can pass themselves off as harmless old folks. No one would ever believe one of our elderly could be capable of such a heinous act."

"Heinous?" Vance skeptically repeated.

"It means atrocious, or monstrous," I offered.

"I know what it means, you knucklehead," Vance grumped. "I simply don't think this crime could be construed as heinous."

"Either way you want to look at it," Jillian continued, "I'm just very glad we got the chest back. I was sick to my stomach after I saw that it was missing."

"How did someone make it into your backroom without you noticing?" I asked.

"Did you see how many people were in Cookbook Nook earlier today?" Jillian challenged. "That reminds me. The store is still going to be hectic. I really should get back. I haven't seen that many people in such close proximity since we went to Disneyland last year, at Christmas time. I will never forget it."

"Why would you willingly go to Disneyland?" Vance asked, genuinely curious. "You two don't have any kids."

"I've always been a Disney fan," I confessed.

Jillian raised her hand and nodded. "Me, too. It's a magical place, Vance. You should take Tori and the girls. I'm sure they'd love it. In fact, why don't we all plan a trip together? Maybe we can see if Harry and Julie could make it."

"What about them?" I asked, as I pointed at Sherlock and Watson's sleeping forms.

"We'd have to get someone to watch them," Jillian admitted.

"It's a shame they don't allow dogs in the park," I said.

Jillian nodded. "That's true, but I've heard they do have a boarding facility at the front gate."

"Meaning, the dogs would have to be in a kennel the entire time we were there. No, I'd never be able to relax if I knew poor Sherlock and Watson had to spend the day cooped up."

"And that's why I love you so much," Jillian said, as she batted her eyes over me. She placed her hand on mine, on top of the table. "Don't ever change."

"I have no intentions of it," I assured her.

"Would you two knock it off?" Vance grumbled. "You guys are in love. I get it. Do you have to make the rest of us go through it with you?"

Jillian rose from the table and squatted down next to Vance, so that she could drape an arm across his shoulders.

"Oh, I get it. You need a hug, don't you?"

Vance's face reddened. "Cut that out."

Jillian giggled and returned to my side. "You blush as easily as Zack does."

"Do not."

"I don't blush," I said, at the same time.

Jillian fixed me with a gaze. "Really? Would you like to amend that statement?"

Vance's face softened and he offered us a smile. "You two really are perfect for each other. I'm glad things are working out so well for you guys."

"That just earned you a hug whether you like it or not," Jillian decided, as she rose to her feet once more. She wrapped her arms around Vance and held the embrace for a few moments. "Thank you. We both appreciate it."

"We really do," I confirmed.

Vance's face was beet red. "All right, all right. Is everyone good? Now, what are we going to do about that thing?"

"I personally think it's time we figured out how to open it," I decided. "This chest was given to me, after all. Wouldn't that suggest whoever sent it thinks I should be able to open it?"

"When are you going to try, Zachary?" Jillian wanted to know.

"This evening. There's currently a class being held at Lentari Cellars right now. Caden has a little more than twenty students following him around."

"What if one of them disguises themselves as a student?" Vance asked.

"I think a senior would kinda stick out in a group of young students," I told my friend. "I've already given Caden a heads-up about the possibility of strangers hanging around the winery. He's going to keep a close eye on everything for me."

Vance nodded. "Good."

"Would you like some help this evening?" Jillian asked. "I can head over to your place once the foot traffic winds down for the day. Usually, the people this festival draws are gone by six p.m."

"What do you mean?" I asked.

Jillian shrugged. "I wish I could explain it. With this particular crowd, after the sun sets, well, so do they. You'd think they were solar-powered."

"Hey, that works for me. If it means you get to come over to my place even sooner than that, then who am I to argue?"

Vance rose to his feet, which woke up the dogs. "Keep me posted, will you?"

"You got it, pal. Sherlock? Watson? Come on. We're taking this thing home."

"Will it be safe there?" Jillian wanted to know.

"I have security cameras everywhere," I explained. "I had originally programmed it to go active once the sun goes down, only I was getting alerted to everything that passed in front of the cameras. So, since I didn't really want to get an email every time a butterfly fluttered by one of the cameras, I've been tinkering with the sensitivity settings. I haven't quite got all the kinks worked out, but it's getting better. I just have to tell the cameras what to look for, and what sounds are acceptable. Right now, I'll take a trigger-happy security system any day of the week."

"So, you'll know when I get there," Jillian said.

"Yep. Come on over when you can, okay?"

We kissed each other goodbye, which had Vance rolling his eyes and heading off to his office. The dogs and I, with the toaster box securely under my arm, headed back to my Jeep. Once we were on the road, I was able to relax.

"We really need to find out what's in this thing once and for all," I told the dogs. "So, if either of you would like to work your magic, feel free, all right?"

The corgis ignored me. I had rolled the back windows down to the halfway point, and both of the dogs were sitting as close as they could to the blowing air. Shrugging, I returned my attention to the box, and what I could do to open it. Clearly, Jillian was right. It was a puzzle box, and one that required a very specific set of instructions to be followed before it would open. However, no one knew what those instructions were. That meant we were going to have to play it by ear.

Back home, the dogs and I were in my office upstairs. As promised, I had activated the motion sensors all over the property. No one would be able to get within a thousand yards of the house without tripping one of the cameras. This was proven by the relentless chirps that were being sent to my phone. And yes, I stopped to check each of them. Most of them were just students moving around the winery. Others were pictures of wild-life, and there were a few that had nothing at all. I'm guessing the blowing wind must have caused a tree branch to sway, which earned it a snapshot from the closest camera.

Oh, well. The added security was worth it.

I sat back in my chair and studied the silver object sitting on my desk. I already knew which pieces on the chest's surface moved, so there really wasn't any point in trying again. It would just be a waste of time. Therefore, it was time to institute Jillian's plan, where I would move one piece at a time, and then check if anything happened. Would the rest of the movable pieces stop moving? Would something new then be able to be moved?

The answer was a very resounding no.

Not to be deterred, since I had only started with the shamrock leaf, I moved to the Scottish thistle. I pressed the stem in, heard it click, and then did my checks. Nothing. I spent the next hour repeating the process for each of the eight moving pieces.

No luck.

Frustrated, I pushed away from my desk. Rising to my feet, I glanced down, looking for the dogs. Not finding them, I moved to my house's second guest bedroom, which had been claimed by the corgis and all their toys. There they were, up on the couch, sound asleep. Squatting down next to them resulted in my knees cracking loudly, which woke up the two of them.

Sherlock regarded me from his upside-down position, while Watson lifted her head to be able to better watch me. I gave each of the dogs a friendly pat before sighing heavily.

"I don't know, guys. Nothing I'm doing is having the slightest bit of effect on this thing. I thought for sure Jillian was on to something, when she suggested the movement of one piece would then allow a completely different piece to move. However, that doesn't seem to be the case."

Sherlock lazily rolled over, until he was laying on the couch with his feet under him. He watched me for a few moments before slowly rising to his feet and giving himself a good shaking, as though there wasn't enough dog hair on that poor sofa.

Sherlock jumped down, shook himself a second time, then looked up at Watson. After a few moments of silence had passed, I watched Watson jump down, give herself her own shake, and then, together, the two corgis trotted out of the room. Curious, I followed. What were those two up to?

We didn't go far. We literally walked out of the room and down the hall, ending up in the room I had just vacated, namely, my office. Both dogs placed themselves before my desk and promptly sat. Catching sight of me watching curiously from the doorway, Sherlock looked up at the top of my desk and let out a low howl.

"Awwooooo."

"And that's supposed to mean *what*?" I wanted to know. "Is there something on my desk you want to look at?"

For the next fifteen minutes, I presented each and every object on my desk—of which there were many—to the corgis, as if looking for their approval. I know what you're thinking. Fifteen minutes? How much crap could I possibly have on my desk? Well, the answer to that was ... a lot.

I have little figurines, statues of dragons holding letter openers, a Bluetooth speaker in the shape of the Millennium Falcon, and a myriad of other knick-knacks, collected from multiple countries. It wasn't until I hit those aforementioned knick-knacks that I got a hit. Well, a *woof*, actually.

Sherlock's ears perked up as I leaned down with one of three crystal paperweights I owned and placed it in front of his nose.

"Awwwwoooooowwoooowwwoooowooo!"

Seriously, I should have known. After all, this particular case was about Ireland, so why shouldn't Sherlock express interest in my Waterford crystal shamrock? I held it out to Watson, only to have her sneeze into my hand.

"Thanks for that, girl. That was properly disgusting. So, let's find out if this is the only thing you're interested in, all right?"

I moved to the dogs' room across the hall. Sure enough, the corgis followed. Placing the crystal shamrock on the small wooden stand that held their 32-inch flat-screen television—hey, don't judge me, it actually keeps them entertained! —I took a couple of steps back and watched. Sherlock and Watson approached the television, sat down, and gazed at the crystal paperweight as though it was the most fascinating thing they had ever seen. Shaking my head, I snatched up my crystal memento of my trip to Cork, Ireland. Then, shrugging, I pulled out my phone and took a picture of the paperweight while it was still in my hand.

"Thanks for that. All-righty-then. You guys are interested in my shamrock. Well, that's not too surprising, is it?"

Why would it be? There is a better than average chance the missing Irish Crown Jewels were sitting in that chest on my desk, just waiting to be discovered. All I had to do was find the key to opening this blasted silver box. Aside from taking a torch to it. If I knew for a fact that cutting the chest open wouldn't harm what was inside, then I would seriously consider it.

My eyes flitted over to my (newly returned) crystal shamrock. The circumstances in which I bought that souvenir suddenly sprang to mind. I had purchased it back in 2009, which was when I first visited Ireland. That particular trip, I remember thinking, was necessary due to a desire to get some hands-on research of Irish castles. Why not make a trip out of it?

Unsurprisingly, it hadn't taken much to convince Samantha, my late wife, to tag along, and together, we spent six glorious days on the Emerald Isle. We explored Cork and Dublin, and even took the time to drive up to Belfast, Northern Ireland, so that we could see the Giant's Causeway. But, I digress. Back to Cork.

While exploring the city, Samantha and I came across the best gift shop we had ever visited: Blarney Woollen. Shirts, trinkets, jewelry, and yes, Waterford crystal, were tastefully displayed from one end of the store to the other. Samantha, understandably, had veered toward the crystal display the instant we entered the store. She selected several vases, a set of dishes, and an angel decoration. Wanting to get something for myself, I had found the small crystal shamrock, which had been perfect.

During the time we had explored the city of Cork, we actually encountered the Chairman of the Cork City Council, which was the equivalent of the city's mayor. Michael O'Connell had invited Sam and me to lunch, and it was there that I revealed to the first person ever, who my alter ego was, and the real reason why we were there, in Cork. Lord Mayor O'Connell then pulled out his cell phone and called his wife, placing the call on speakerphone. He asked Cara to tell him the name of the book she was reading. After revealing she had become captivated with *Through The Fog*, a novel by none other than Chastity Wadsworth, Mayor O'Connell himself became our personal tour guide for the rest of the time we were in Cork, which floored me. Surely, the mayor of a city the size of Cork would have something better to do?

Then, on the last day of our visit, the Lord Mayor explained his actions. He was just repaying a favor, he explained, because ever since *Through The Fog* had been published, tourism in Cork had increased by nearly 300 percent! Now, there was no proof that it was all due to a book I had written, but seeing how I had set the book's location in Ireland, and the year in question was the same year it had been published, well, it had been an easy assumption to make.

Coming back to the present, I looked down at Sherlock, and then back at the crystal shamrock. What did Mayor O'Connell tell me the day we left? That if there was ever anything he could do for me, then all I had to do was ask?

My eyes jumped over to the chest and the Celtic shamrock on its front. Well, I was pretty certain Michael was no longer the mayor, since he revealed those positions were chosen on an annual basis. But, what could it hurt to try?

I reached for my cell and, after a few moments of searching, found the number I had long ago saved into my contact book.

"Office of the Chairman of Cork City Council, this is Clodagh, how can I help you?"

"Hello, Clodagh. My name is Zachary Anderson. I was looking to reach a man by the name of Michael O'Connell, who used to be the Lord Mayor of Cork. Now, I know he isn't anymore, but I was wondering if there was a way you could ..."

"Michael O'Connell?" the woman hesitantly repeated. "You're looking for Mr. O'Connell?"

"Oh, good. Do you know him?"

"I should say so, sir. He's my uncle."

"Really? It's definitely a small world. Listen, I met your uncle in 2009. He told me that, if I ever needed a favor, I was to let him know. Well, I've got something to run by him. Is there any way I could get you to give me his number?"

"The best I could do, sir, is take your number and give it to my uncle. If he so chooses, then he would call you."

"That'll do, Clodagh. Thank you."

I gave the girl my name and number. After a moment's hesitation, I gave her the *other* name.

"You also go by a woman's name?" Clodagh incredulously asked.

"It's a nom de plume. Silly, I know. He'll know who it is."

"I will give him the message," Clodagh promised.

"Thank you. Hey, out of curiosity, what time is it there? It has to be getting late, right?"

"Well, it *is* evening, Mr. Anderson. This office closes at nine p.m. Your accent. Is it American?"

"Yes. I live in Oregon. Er, it's a state in the Pacific Northwest, in the U.S.A."

"Ah. Very well. I will relay the message."

Clodagh must have immediately phoned her uncle, because my cell was ringing in less than five minutes.

"Hello?"

"Mr. Anderson? It's Michael O'Connell. It's good to hear from you! Apparently, you called my niece earlier, looking for me?"

"I did. I'm sorry to bother you at home, especially when it's late," I began.

"Oh, don't you worry about a thing. That offer I made to you years ago still stands, my friend. I am intrigued. What can I do for you?"

"I've been doing a bit of research, and stumbled across something I was hoping you'd be able to shed some light on."

"Research for a new book, I presume? Do tell. What did you need help with?"

"The Irish Crown Jewels."

"Ah. Such a travesty. It never would have happened under my watch. What would you like to know about them?"

Taking a deep breath, I decided to just plow forward. "Have the jewels ever been associated with any type of symbol?"

Michael was silent for so long that I had to check the phone—twice—to verify I was still connected.

"Michael? Are you still there?"

"What would you ask me such a thing for, Mr. Anderson? Is there something you need to tell me?"

"I will answer you, but only if you answer me first."

"Very well. You want to know about our crown jewels? As you may very well know, they were stolen in 1907 and never recovered."

"I do know that," I admitted.

"Did you know that those jewels were stored in a silver chest commissioned especially for them?"

It was my turn to fall silent.

"You knew that already, didn't you?" Michael surmised. "May I ask *how*?"

"Tell me about this chest first," I pleaded.

"The chest. Well, it was designed by a Japanese immigrant who wanted to find a way to secure the jewels."

My eyes found Sherlock, who had been staring at me with what could only be described as a smug smile on his face. How? How could that dog have known I could get so many answers just by picking up the phone?

"It's a puzzle box, isn't it?"

"Mr. Anderson?" Michael slowly and *carefully* asked. "Are you in possession of this chest?"

"Well, Michael, there's a chance I am. Now, about this special symbol of yours. Will you tell me about it?"

"This chest that you have in your possession, it has this symbol you're asking me about?"

"It does."

"I'm finding it hard to believe you. Tell me what you see, and I'll tell you if it matches the description I know."

"Please, Michael," I implored, "just tell me. I've already had several people try to steal it. I just want to figure out what it is and then get it back to its rightful owner."

"Wait, what?"

"Hmm?"

"Mr. Anderson, am I to understand you plan on returning this ... forgive me. If what you have in your possession turns out to be the actual *stolen* Irish Crown Jewels, you're telling me your intent is to return them?"

"Well, they don't belong to me now, do they?" I pointed out.

"It's a shamrock," Michael finally answered. "And, it's a knot, woven together to form that shamrock. Is that … is it what you see?"

"Yes."

"By all the saints! What … how … where …?"

"It showed up at my door, Michael. That's all I'll say about it. I'm trying to open it now. If your missing jewelry is inside, then I'll be needing your help in returning it."

"Of course! This … this may be the leverage I need to have another go as Lord Mayor!"

"Looking to serve another term?" I asked.

"Indubitably. The announcement of the return of our jewels would be all the publicity I need in order to secure another term."

"Glad to know I could help out," I joked.

"Now, on to serious matters," Michael said, as his voice dropped and became stern. "You mentioned someone tried to steal the chest. Is this true?"

"Yep. We're dealing with the Forces of STUPID here."

"The forces of stupid?" Michael repeated, puzzled. "I'm not sure what you mean."

"Wait. I keep calling them by the wrong acronym. I'm trying to remember what it stood for. Ah, I've got it. They claim to be the Strategic Team of Patriotic Irish Descendants."

"Oh, by heaven, not *them*," Michael moaned.

"You've heard of them? Are they someone I need to worry about?"

"They're committed, that's for sure," Michael confirmed. "Thankfully, they're amateurs. They're disorganized, clumsy, and not very resourceful. Is this not so? Have you seen something that suggests otherwise?"

"No," I said, laughing, "that totally confirms what I've witnessed over here. I just don't want them to get desperate and try something that they're going to regret. We already captured one of their group, but he escaped when he was in the hospital."

"My word," Michael breathed, "what have you been doing with your spare time?"

"You wouldn't believe me, pal. So, before I go, I have to ask. Is there a known way to open this chest?"

"No, I'm afraid not. The last person who knew the secret died in 1974."

"It was a shared secret?" I asked.

"Known only to the Order of Saint Patrick," Michael confirmed. "The jewels were created in 1831 for the Sovereign and Grand Master of the Order of Saint Patrick. The jewels were brought out and worn whenever a new knight was ordained. Those jewels, along with the collars of five knights of the order, were stolen from Dublin Castle. If those jewels are recovered ..."

"And?" I inquired, after Michael had trailed off. "What about it? If those jewels are recovered, what then?"

"I would imagine the people of Ireland will have some celebrating to do, and it'll be all thanks to you."

I automatically looked down at the dogs. "Believe it or not, I can't take all the credit. My two *assistants* are the ones who pointed me in your direction."

"Your assistants?" Michael skeptically repeated.

"You heard that right. I'll explain later, provided everything pans out the way I think it's going to."

"You lead a very interesting life, Mr. Anderson."

"You don't know the half of it. All right, I'll get working on this chest. I'll keep you posted."

"Please do, Mr. Anderson. Good day to you."

"And a good evening to you, too."

Hanging up, I looked down at the dogs and shook my head. I pulled out the middle desk drawer on my right and selected several treats from the extensive stash I kept there. From a writer's point-of-view, if you're in the zone, and the words are flowing so fast your fingers can barely keep up, the last thing you'll want is to be yanked out by one of your dogs. Therefore, a drawer full of distractions was a good thing to have nearby.

"Good job, guys. That was incredibly helpful. The Order of Saint Patrick, huh? And the chest was created by a Japanese immigrant. That means Jil-

JEFFREY POOLE

lian was right. There's a very specific set of steps we need to take in order to open that blasted thing."

Right on cue, my cell phone chirped. Glancing at the display, I saw that it was a proximity alarm from my security system. A car had just pulled into my driveway.

"Look at that, guys. Jillian is here! Wow, wait a moment. What time is it?"

For the record, it was later than I thought, but much earlier than I expected to see my fiancée. Either way, Jillian's arrival was a good thing. I was going to need her help in order to figure out the steps necessary to open the chest.

The three of us headed downstairs, just in time to see Jillian walking up the steps.

"Hello, Zachary! What ... you've learned something! What is it? What happened? What did you find out?"

"I didn't say a darn thing. How could you possibly know that?"

Jillian placed a soft, cool hand on the side of my face. "You're flushed with excitement. I can feel the heat radiating from your face. So, tell me!"

"I spoke with former Lord Mayor Michael O'Connell, of County Cork, Ireland."

"Today?" Jillian asked, as she stepped inside and took off her coat. I promptly hung it on a peg just inside the door. "Someone from Ireland called you?"

"I called him," I clarified, "but not until Sherlock suggested I should."

Jillian looked down at the tri-colored corgi and ruffled his fur. Then, she did the same for Watson.

"Well, isn't that a smart boy? Good for you, Sherlock. Umm, can I ask how he did that?"

"Come upstairs," I said. "We've got lots to do."

Returning to my study, I pulled a folding chair out of the closet and set it next to my desk. Patting the seat, I pulled out my phone, intent on reviewing the pictures I had taken since this crazy case started.

"I was wondering when we would start looking at the pictures," Jillian said, once she was sitting beside me. She waited for me to locate the start of the corgi clues and, once I had passed the phone to her, she studied the image. "So, what are we looking at?"

I leaned toward Jillian and glanced down. "The elderly couple from Vance's house. Do you see this lady, right here? Granted, I wasn't able to capture her face too well, but this is the one who planted the bug on Watson's collar. Additionally, she's the one who had the chest strapped to the back of her little scooter."

"Ah. And here's the shamrock, from the front of the chest. Hmm, that's odd."

"What is?" I wanted to know.

Jillian tapped the screen. "Why wouldn't you have taken a picture of the shamrock first? Why start with the old man and woman?"

"Because," I explained, "the first picture was

taken before the chest even arrived. This was probably about half an hour before I opened the crate to find *that*."

"Interesting. Let's see who's next. Here we have ... the Bradigan sisters. Why did you take their picture?"

I pointed down at the dogs. "They're the ones who perked up as they passed by. Trust me, I wish those two could talk. I'd love to know what they were thinking."

"Did they perk up for everyone?" Jillian wanted to know.

"No, only select people."

"These were taken at the céilí, weren't they?" Jillian asked, as she swiped my phone's display to bring up the next set of pictures. "I can see that you've taken pictures of some people, and not of others. Should I assume these are the persons Sherlock and Watson were watching?"

I nodded. "That's exactly right. I wish I knew why."

Jillian was silent as she scrolled between the five or six pictures I took while I was at her Irish-themed party. Wait. Irish-themed? Was that the link?

"How well do you know the people in the pictures?" I eagerly asked. "Look. There's the one of Tori and her pendant."

"Waterford," Jillian said, nodding. "More Irish themes."

"And here we have ... I don't know. I don't know

who this is, or who's in the next one, for that matter."

"Let me see. Well, here's a picture of the O'Sullivans. They're Irish, obviously. And, of course, we have Aine and Saoirse Bradigan. They were also born in Ireland."

"What about the next two?" I asked. "I didn't recognize them."

I watched as Jillian scrolled to the next picture. This one was of a woman in her forties, wearing a formal dress, complete with glittering studded earrings and a wide, shimmering necklace. My eyes alternated between the earrings and the necklace as a thought occurred.

"Go to the next one, would you?"

Jillian complied, and a second picture of an unknown woman appeared.

"Do we know who this is?" I asked.

Jillian shook her head. "No, I'm sorry. I'm just trying to figure out why you took a picture. Oh, I mean, why the dogs showed an interest and you ended up taking her picture."

I tapped the screen, directly over the woman's throat, where a very prominent set of jewelry could be seen.

"There's our answer. The dogs were zeroing in on jewelry. Look at the last picture. Do you see that necklace? That thing looks incredibly gaudy."

"It's a bib necklace," Jillian explained. "Think of them like showpieces. Oh! I think I see what you mean. Since this whole ordeal is focusing on the stolen Irish Crown Jewels, you think that's why Sherlock and Watson were paying attention to fancy jewelry?"

"That's my running theory," I admitted. "But … the Bradigan sisters? Look. They aren't wearing … never mind. They're Irish. That's why the dogs perked up."

"We're making progress," Jillian said, delighted. "Let's see what else you have."

I took the phone back and scooted closer to Jillian. Both corgis, I might add, lifted their heads to give the two of us neutral looks. I waggled a finger at them.

"Back to sleep, guys. We're still going through your clues, so no input is required, thank you very much."

"I'd say it's fairly clear what the dogs were trying to show us."

"Ireland."

"Yes. They focused on anything having to do with Ireland, including anyone who had on gaudy jewelry."

"I've seen the pics of the stolen jewels," I reported. "They're gaudy, too. Hey, I think we're getting better at this!"

"Or, more likely," Jillian argued, "is that Sherlock and Watson are making the clues easier for us to decipher."

That sobered me. I heard an exasperated snort as both dogs resumed their napping. Condescending little boogers. That had better not be what they were doing.

"Next up is ... ah. Here we go. Talk about the slowest chase in the history of chases."

"This is the group of seniors you were following?" Jillian asked, leaning close. "They certainly look harmless, don't they?"

"You should have seen them split after I took back the chest. Oh, there we go. I pretended I heard a ringing phone, and when I pulled mine out, I took their picture. Wow, could they move when they wanted to."

"And they left their canes and scooters," Jillian observed. "What's this? Is this another shamrock?"

I pointed at the crystal paperweight a mere two feet away, on the surface of my desk.

"There it is, right there. That picture was taken just a little bit earlier. The dogs came out of their room and stopped right there, to stare up at it."

Jillian hefted the shamrock in her hand. "Is this Waterford, too?"

"It is. I bought it in Cork."

"I envy you, Zachary. Ireland is on my Bucket List."

"Not for long," I reminded her, which had her hugging me tight. "Speaking of Ireland, when I reached out to my friend, the former mayor of Cork, Michael identified that chest. He confirmed it was the final resting place of the Irish Crown Jewels."

"Oooo! So, that means they're in there? How

wonderful! We need to figure out how to open this thing!"

"Before I reached out to Michael, I spent over an hour on the chest, trying your suggestion."

"What suggestion?" Jillian asked.

I slid my notepad over to her. "This one. You said we should treat it like a Japanese puzzle box. Moving one piece should unlock something different, or allow another piece to move even further or, perhaps, in a different direction. I tried all eight moving parts. Nothing happened."

"Oh, I'm sorry. I really thought I was on to something."

"You were," I confirmed. "Michael informed me that the person who made that chest was Japanese. Do you know what that means? You were right! There've got to be some very specific steps we need to take in order to get that thing open."

Jillian was silent as she studied markings and symbols on the silver box. She leaned forward, experimentally twisted the top left corner, and then tried a few other combinations. Nothing worked. Just then, she lifted the chest and, holding it aloft, looked at me.

"May I?"

"May you *what*?" I wanted to know.

Jillian turned and lowered the chest down to the floor. As if they had been personally called over to give it an inspection, both corgis appeared and began sniffing the chest. After a few moments, Sherlock stopped and touched his nose to the chest's surface.

"What'd he touch?" I eagerly asked, growing excited.

"Just the corner," Jillian said, giving out a dejected sigh. "There must have been something on my finger, so when I … Zachary? Sherlock is sniffing again. Look! He touched the thistle!"

I hurriedly slid the notepad back over and made a few notes. "Anything else?"

"It doesn't look like it."

"What if," I began, "instead of finding the first step, which would unlock the next, what if we have to move *two* pieces before the second step is revealed?"

"The corner and the thistle," Jillian said, amazed. "May I?"

"Go ahead," I urged.

Jillian twisted the corner once more, and then pressed down on the thistle's stem. For all intents and purposes, it looked as though nothing had changed. I looked at Jillian and held up my hands in a *now what* gesture.

"Let's try to move the … Zachary! The shamrock! The petal isn't moving!"

"What? It was just a moment ago. Let me see. No, you're right. What about the sun? Or the horses?"

"Let me see. No! Those aren't moving, either! What do you think that means?"

Before I could answer, both dogs surged to their feet and began snarling. Staring down at the dogs, with surprise written all over my face, I was about to ask them what the problem was, when I suddenly heard a chirp from my phone. A quick glance at the camera confirmed that the front door had opened.

"That's the front door," I quietly whispered. "Someone just came inside!"

"We're already here, Mr. Anderson," an angry voice snapped, from the doorway behind us. "That'll be far enough. We'll take that chest now, thank you very much. We appreciate you taking the time to locate it for us. I cannot begin to tell you how long we've searched for it."

Two armed figures appeared in the hall, outfitted entirely in black. Sweatshirts, pants, shoes, and even sunglasses were all black. Plus, both assailants had their hoodies pulled up and over their heads. Fabric face masks, like the kind someone would wear if they didn't want to breathe in someone else's germs, stretched from nose to chin. Wearing both mask and sunglasses, no part of their faces were exposed. However, one thing I could determine was that we were looking at a male and a female, and I was willing to bet the female was the one who kept changing her appearance through the use of different wigs. In fact, if I looked closely at the person I suspected to be a woman, I could see wisps of long, red hair poking through her hoodie and her mask.

The woman strode confidently up to me, pointed at the chest on the floor, and motioned with her gun for me to hand it to her. Once it was tucked under her arm, and after hearing the dogs growl once more, the gun was aimed at the corgis. Or, more specifically, at Sherlock.

"Quiet, boy. We'll get it back. Don't forget, we're dealing with STUPID people here."

"We're holding the guns," the male sneered. "I'd watch it if I were you. If you try to come after us, we'll shoot." The man looked at his companion. "Go. Get that thing in the car and get it started."

The woman nodded and disappeared through the door. We heard her hurry down the stairs and then, a few moments later, an engine was fired up. The guy began backstepping out the door. As soon as he was in the hall, he closed the door to my office and hurriedly knocked over a nearby bookcase, thereby blocking us in our room. Then, we heard the guy sprint down the stairs. As the two of us rose to our feet, we heard several gunshots in the distance. What was he shooting at?

Opening my office door (it swung *in* not *out*), I verified they were gone before helping Jillian and dogs out of the room.

## TEN

H ow could this be happening?" I demanded, as I rushed outside. "How did they even know we had the flippin' thing in there?"

"I'm more concerned about them getting it opened," Jillian said, from somewhere behind me. As we bolted down the stairs, we came to a stop at an empty driveway. "Tell me you have an idea where they might have gone?"

We both slowly turned in place. There was no sign of any other vehicle anywhere. Even if their car *was* out of sight, it shouldn't have been out of earshot. Living out in the country as I do, the approach—or departure—of any type of vehicle can be heard for miles. Neither of us heard a thing, I'm sorry to say.

"Look, Zachary! Look at what they did to our cars!"

My Jeep had two flats, as did Jillian's SUV. I paced around the cars as I angrily scolded myself for being so careless. One thing was clear: I hadn't given these STUPID people enough credit. They were more organized, better prepared, and better informed than I was led to believe. Somehow, they managed to sneak onto my property and make it through my own front door before my so-called security system could indicate something was amiss.

Sherlock and Watson skirted around the now disabled cars and pulled us toward the garage.

"What are they doing?" Jillian wanted to know.

I suddenly grinned. I had forgotten that, thanks to Jillian, I was now the owner of *two* cars. I should've known that *they* wouldn't have forgotten that. Punching the code on the keypad, I watched the garage door as it rumbled upward.

"You're not suggesting we try to follow them in *that*, are you?" Jillian asked, using a tone dripping with skepticism. "Zachary, this isn't the 1940s. The person who stole the chest is going to have something a lot more powerful than this."

The garage's fluorescent lights made the dark, forest green paint sparkle on my 1930 Ruxton Model C sedan. A gift from Jillian, after learning the car had come with a house she had purchased last year, the car had been meticulously restored. However, the caveat to that is that it would probably *stay* restored only if I could remember where each of the car's three gears were located.

The dogs were waiting by the rear passenger door. Lifting Their Royal Canineships up into the classic automobile, I risked a glance at my fiancée and was rewarded with seeing her already in the passenger seat.

"Remember, reverse is in first position," Jillian warned, as if she had been reading my mind.

"I never should have told you about how I dented the bumper," I chuckled, as I eased the classic piece of automotive history out of the garage.

The Ruxton Model C sedan is a very rare car that most people, like myself prior to owning one, have probably never heard of. Before picking up the keys to this beauty, I had no idea what it was, only that every picture I had ever seen of it made me think of Al Capone, Bugsy Malone, and other mobsters from that era. The car was gorgeous, had only required a minimal amount of effort to restore, and as a result, I had people asking to buy it on a daily basis.

In this particular case, we didn't have the time to stop to allow admirers to take its picture. We had a thief to find, and we had to do so before they could skip town. Jillian was right. I was pretty sure we had been only moments away from opening the chest and determining, once and for all, whether or not the missing Irish Crown Jewels could finally be reported as found. We were on track to do just that, but, before we could, we were given one mother of a reality check.

Two people had entered my house. Two people

made it up the stairs and caught us unprepared, brandishing guns. One of them, I was certain, was the woman with the bright-red hair. I was also certain it was the same woman who had slipped the GPS tracking bug onto Watson's collar. In fact, it was also the same lady who had donned a frizzy white wig and swiped the chest a few days ago, and ended up being caught, on one of those scooters.

How? That's what I wanted to know. How had this person made it onto my property, when I had every square inch of the driveway covered? I had no fewer than three different cameras covering my front door, yet somehow, this woman made it all the way inside my house. What had I missed? Had this lady used some type of high-tech device to defeat my security system?

"Penny for your thoughts?"

I glanced over at the passenger seat. "I'm just thinking how disgusted I am with my security system. I was so sure that we'd be fine. After all, cameras are everywhere, and the security stickers on the front door should have been enough of a deterrent to ward off anyone stupid enough to try sneaking up on us."

"I'd be talking to the company that installed it," Jillian said, frowning. "There should be some type of … what's with that face? Who did you use? Zachary Michael, tell me you didn't install it yourself."

"The instructions said that anyone could do it," I argued. "I figured, why not save a little money?"

"You bought a do-it-yourself security system?" Jillian asked, incredulous.

"When you say it like that, then yeah, it sounds foolish. Trust me, I'll be rectifying *that* little problem just as soon as I'm able to."

"I'm surprised you didn't get a security system like the one we had installed in Monterey."

During a much-needed vacation to Monterey, California, we ended up having a more adventurous time than we had planned and doing a huge favor for a famous, nearby aquarium.

"I thought about it," I admitted, as I twisted the Ruxton's shifting knob and eased the car into second gear. "As I'm sure you remember, that particular system was state-of-the-art: mobile access, remote arm and disarm, and offline data storage. That cost us a pretty penny."

"It was worth it," Jillian reminded me. "And, isn't this? This is the world you created here, Zachary. I would have thought that a simple price tag wouldn't have made a difference to you, not when those you love are at stake."

I turned to see Jillian batting her eyes at me. Then, I noticed both dogs were watching me in the rearview mirror. Laughing, I threw up my hands.

"Fine. You guys all win. I'll make the call tomorrow morning. Satisfied?"

Sherlock and Watson settled down, into the plush seats, just as we merged onto South State Road, heading west.

"Come on, guys. Don't get comfy. We're tracking the bad guys! Aren't you two supposed to be poking your noses through the window? You know, making doggie nose art all over the glass?"

Sherlock had the audacity to lower his head until it was resting on his paws. After a few moments, his eyes closed and the little corgi was snoring. Watson snuggled close to her packmate and, before long, she was out like a light, too.

"What's with those two?" Jillian asked.

"I wish I knew. You know, I have no idea where we're going, or what we're looking for.

"If we did," Jillian began, as she pulled out her phone, "I could have the entire town looking for it. I'll bet we could find it in less time that it takes to get to the police station."

I nodded. "If we knew the make and model, sure. The police station? That's a good place to start. I wonder if Vance is there?"

Jillian held up her phone. "He is. I've given him a brief recap of what's happened. He's not too happy about the theft of the chest, but that's not too surprising. I think he really wanted to find out what was in it."

"I still hope to be able to tell him," I said, as I noticed the first sign telling me that, in less than three miles, we'd be entering Pomme Valley's city limits. "I still can't believe I let them manage to slip inside the house, unnoticed. I didn't get any alerts or notices. This is all my fault."

Jillian placed her soft hand over mine. "It's not

your fault, Zachary. These are extenuating circumstances. Let's just focus on figuring out where
the red-haired woman went."

I looked back at the mirror, at the sleeping
corgis, and scowled. "Sherlock? Watson? I could
really use you guys right about now. They know
the first step in getting the chest open. We need to
find it before they get it all the way open."

"For all we know, they'll destroy the chest just
to get at the jewelry inside," Jillian said.

"Not helping," I grumbled. "Guys? What do you
say?"

Sherlock cracked open an eye and looked at me
in the mirror. After a few moments, the feisty little corgi rose to his feet, stretched his back, and
then raised himself into a seated position. Good.
He was now looking out the window. Was he trying to tell us something?

Sherlock gave himself a good shaking and then
looked at me, as though I needed to discover the
next step on my own. When I didn't say anything,
Sherlock let out a low *woof*. Watson woke, looked
over at her packmate, and then noticed he was
looking at me. Just like that, I had two corgis staring at me. Sherlock woofed again.

"What is he woofing at?" Jillian wanted to
know.

"I'm not sure. What's up, pal? What do you
need?"

Sherlock surprised me by lunging forward so
that his front end was on my arm rest. He lowered

his snout and then nudged my phone. The tri-colored corgi looked up at me, snorted, and then at Jillian. He nudged my phone a second time, knocking it out of the cup holder. Jillian quickly retrieved it but held it up in front of the corgi.

"What's the matter, Sherlock? Is there something on the phone that you want to see?"

Sherlock stretched forward and nudged the phone again, almost dislodging it from Jillian's hand.

"All right, is there something you want *me* to see?"

There was another nudge.

"How about Zack? Is there something you want him to look at?"

"Awwooooo!"

Surprised, I took my eyes off the road long enough to stare at my phone. What was on it that my dog wanted me to see? Then, I had to laugh at myself. If only a therapist could hear me say that, then I'd most certainly have a date with a shrink on a weekly basis.

Exasperated, Sherlock woofed, and nudged the phone a final time. This time, somehow, he had activated the generic app I had downloaded so I could view the footage of the security camera online. Both Jillian and I came to the same conclusion at the exact same time.

"Your security system!" Jillian exclaimed.

"I can look at the footage online," I said, shaking my head. "I should have checked to see if it picked up anything. I just assumed it didn't."

"Can you walk me through how to do it?" Jillian said, as she stared at the unfamiliar app.

"I wish I could. It has a strange setup. I'd have to …"

"Zachary!" Jillian cried. "Pull over! Right here. Pull over!"

I complied, and brought the Ruxton to as rapid a stop as I could. We were currently in PV city limits, and there was a row of houses on either side of the street. Both dogs, I noticed, were standing up on their back legs, looking out the right-side window.

"What is it?"

Jillian pointed at a very familiar house on the corner of the closest intersection. Parked in the driveway was one sky-blue Corvette Stingray.

"Okay, so, it's Dottie's house. What about it?"

Jillian was already on her way out of the car. She pointed at the driveway and it dawned on me what she wanted me to do. Shrugging, I parked my classic car next to Dottie's, er, classic car. Dottie was already exiting the house as I pulled the dogs out.

"Hi, guys!" Dottie said, as she emerged from her house. She had a dishtowel in her hands and it looked as though she had been in the middle of cleaning her house. "Can I help you with something?"

"No time to explain," Jillian said, as she pointed at the Vette. "Could we borrow that? We need to catch a thief and it's not going to happen in *that*!"

Dottie's eyebrows shot up. "Another chase? You guys live such exciting lives! Sure, I'll go get the keys."

As soon as our friend was holding out the keys to her sportscar, Jillian surprised me by snatching them out of Dottie's hand. She placed her hand on my chest and pointed at the driver's seat.

"Nuh-uh. *I* am driving. You do your thing with your phone and tell me what we're looking for. I'll take care of the rest."

Bemused by the entire situation, I could only nod. Ushering the dogs inside the blue Corvette, I slid onto the passenger seat and had just managed to close the door when the Vette roared to life. I remembered something Jillian had told me, and it came slamming back into me at full force. My fiancée may have been born here, in Pomme Valley, but she once said Michael, her late husband, told her she drove like she had lived in Southern California her entire life.

In the blink of an eye, Jillian had the Vette up to 50 mph, and it felt like she hadn't even shifted out of second gear yet. Surprised, it was all I could do to hang on. Risking a glance back at the dogs, I could see that they had their tongues out, and if the windows had been open, I'm sure their heads would have been sticking out, regardless of our velocity.

"Zachary? Your phone. You're supposed to be

looking for our thief."

"Right. Sorry. You surprised me, that's all."

"You're referring to my driving?"

"Uh, yeah. Sorry."

"In this case, it's better to drive aggressively than like a ... a ..."

"... grandpa?" I finished for her, with a grin.

Jillian giggled. "Your words, not mine. Now, what do you have?"

I pulled my phone out and started the tedious log-in process to access my online account. As soon as I was at my account page, I followed the necessary steps to enter the *Storage Locker*, where all uploaded files were kept, and began sorting them into chronological order. I found the correct file on the third attempt. Watching time elapse as I kept an eye on the feed which had my driveway, I had let thirteen minutes go by before the file ended prematurely. Surprised, I played the file again, and jumping it forward to the 12:55 mark, I watched as a car appeared in the frame. However, a split second later, the file ended.

And *that* was the last file that was uploaded to my account. My limited technical skills were able to engage long enough to spit out an answer as to why I hadn't received any notices: the security system wasn't connected to the Internet. But, that was exactly when that car appeared? Had it passed my driveway, or had it simply been bad luck that my Internet connection dropped at that exact time?

A nagging thought occurred. The internet goes down just when I need it most? I'd like to think that, if the driver of that car had done something to my internet connection, then it would have, at least, been able to take his picture. It's not like he was there earlier, and ... wait. Someone *had* been out to my place before. Someone *could* have set some type of device at the point where my house connected to my internet service provider. Whether it's a phone line or a coaxial cable, there's always one junction point where, if you trace the cable from the pole, you'll see where it connects to a house.

If our good buddy Ernest, the shady guy who'd broken into the winery, managed to place some type of device that, when triggered, would have disconnected my ISP with my house, then that would most certainly have prevented the cameras from uploading pictures and video to the internet. That also meant that the cameras must have the photographs and video stored locally, on their internal memory, and were just waiting for the internet connection to be restored. However, that didn't do me any good at the moment. I needed that video *now*.

Going backward, frame by frame, I froze the video at the moment the car appeared at the head of my driveway. I saved the picture and forwarded it to both Jillian and Vance. My detective friend must have been waiting by his phone, because I had a response in less than five seconds.

THIS IS WHO WE'RE LOOKING FOR?

Assuring him that the small, blue hatchback was, most certainly, involved in some fashion, Vance told me he was going to send out an APB for the car. Jillian briefly glanced at the picture as we approached downtown PV. She nodded and gave me an encouraging smile.

"So, that's how they did it."

I turned to study the picture for a few moments. "That's how they did *what*?"

"That's how they got away. No wonder." Jillian wove through traffic better than any professional driver. Screeching and honking sounded as we hurried toward the police station. "That looks like a Toyota Prius."

"So?"

"That means it's a hybrid. More than likely, they weren't using the gasoline engine."

My eyes widened with surprise and I snapped my fingers. "Of course! That's why we didn't hear them. Their car was running virtually silent. Still, there was no sign of them at all. You've seen my driveway. It's at least three hundred feet long. How could they have made it down that in the time it took for us to run outside?"

Jillian suddenly groaned aloud. Concerned, I checked the surroundings. I didn't see anything alarming so, questioningly, I turned to her and waited for an explanation.

"The answer to that was they didn't have to.

What did we do? We ran outside and *assumed* they drove off."

"Oh, son of a biscuit eater," I growled, letting out my own groan. "They were still at the winery, weren't they? They probably drove their car out to the backside of the winery or maybe the warehouse."

Armed with the new information, I sent it off to Vance. I even sent along the description of the woman I believed to be the driver. As expected, I got a snarky response.

HOW MANY TIMES HAVE I TOLD YOU NOT TO JUMP TO ANY CONCLUSIONS? DOES THAT MEAN THEY'RE BEHIND YOU NOW?

I read the message to Jillian, who, surprised, checked the mirrors, as though a Prius would have been able to keep up with a 1967 Corvette Coupe sportscar.

"I don't see anything back there."

"That means they could still be anywhere," I complained. "This keeps getting better and better. We played right into their hands, didn't we?"

Jillian sadly nodded. "We did, but don't count us out yet. We have *them*."

I twisted to look back at the dogs. Both Sherlock and Watson were resting, Sphinx-like, in the storage compartment behind the two seats.

Less than two minutes later, we turned right and headed north, up 6th Street. As we approached E Street, I felt the Vette slow, but only marginally.

Holy cow! Jillian was gonna make the sportscar drift around the corner! How cool!

"What's with that face?" Jillian asked.

"I'm waiting for us to go drifting around that corner," I said, as I pointed at the intersection of 6th and E.

"I am so *not* drifting this car," Jillian retorted. The brakes were engaged, and I finally felt the mechanical beast slow. "Aggressive driving is dangerous."

"Says the person who was weaving through traffic as though we weren't allowed to go below 50."

Jillian nodded. "*Speed.* Great movie, but don't get me started about that bus. There's no *way* it could have made the jump across an incomplete freeway."

"And that's why I love you so much," I grinned, like a lovestruck teenager.

We turned left, and headed west on E Street, toward the police department. As we skidded to a stop in front of the station, we saw that Vance was already there, on the curb. He was pacing and, unsurprisingly, on the phone.

"Yes, sir," he was saying, as I rolled the window down. "We're looking for a blue Prius. Driver? Rumored to be a red-headed woman. No sir, we don't have a picture."

My eyes widened as I realized that yes, there was a photo of the driver. When I took her picture several days ago, she had been wearing a white, frizzy wig. But, the picture did show her face in clear, high-definition, I might add. I quickly sent the picture to Vance, who glanced at his phone to identify the nature of the alert. Seeing that it was from me, I watched him tap the screen and then hold the phone up to his face. Incredulously, he turned to me.

"Wait a moment, sir. Zack? Who's this?"

"That's the lady who was driving one of those scooters from a few nights ago. Put some red hair on her and you'll have our driver!"

"You rock, Zack! Captain? Did you hear that? I'm sending you a picture Zack took a few days ago. The driver is the lady with the white hair. She's now wearing some type of red wig that ... scratch that. We don't know what color hair is natural for her. Could be white, could be red, you never know. Yes sir, we'll keep you posted." Finishing the call, Vance turned to us and squatted down, so he could look at us through the window. "This lady? The one with the white hair? Or, better yet, the one who now has red hair. Who is she?"

"She's the one who was outside your house earlier this week," I reminded my friend. "She's the one who ..."

" ... bugged Watson," Vance finished for me. "I'll be damned. Of the three times you've seen her now, has she ever disguised her face?"

Both Jillian and I were shaking our heads.

"No. The only thing I remember seeing that was different each time was her hair. Granted, this time she was wearing a face mask and sunglasses, but parts of her hair were peaking through the mask, and that hair was red."

Vance was tapping something into his phone, undoubtedly updating someone about the thief.

"Shouldn't the police be setting out roadblocks?" Jillian asked. "They must still be in town. In fact, hold on. Let's see if PV would be willing to help."

Vance and I watched as Jillian pulled her phone out, saved the picture of the Prius I had sent her, and sent it out in a single message. All in all, it took her less than ten seconds. Certain that she had more to do than just that, I pointed at her blinged-out purple phone.

"That's it? What did you do? I thought you wanted to send that picture out to more than just one person."

"I did. I sent it to everyone in my phone."

"How?" both Vance and I echoed.

"You should look up *Groups* and how to use them," Jillian informed us. She looked at me and smiled. "In short, you can create a new contact on your phone, specify you're creating a group, and then add users to that group. Then, when you send out a message, you tell it you want to send to the group, and the phone takes care of the rest."

"Amazing," I decided.

"Incredible," Vance added. "I need to do that with all the contacts on my phone. Officers, techs, I.T. guys, and so on. I must have close to a thousand people on my phone."

I shrugged. "Yeah, sure. Me, too."

I got the sense that we were about to hold a popularity contest when both dogs were suddenly on their feet and looking out the front windshield, which meant they were looking west, onto E Street. Did they notice something? Or, perhaps, smell something?

"What's with them?" Vance wanted to know.

I shrugged. "I'm not sure. Well, while we're waiting for Jillian's master list of operatives to report in," Jillian giggled for this, "let's see what master sleuths Sherlock and Watson have up their furry sleeves."

Setting both dogs down on the sidewalk running alongside E Street, I was about to ask Jillian how often she added someone to her group when I felt a tug on the leash. Looking down, I saw that the corgis were about to morph into their Clydesdale personas and do their best to pull me down the street. Gently reining them in, I looked back at Jillian, and then Vance, and pointed west.

"Methinks we be going *that* way, little lady."

"Do they smell something?" Vance hopefully asked.

"I'm not really sure," I answered, adopting a serious tone. "If they ever learn English, or become telepathic, then I'll be sure to let you know."

Vance snorted with irritation. "You know, there was a time when you weren't so sarcastic."

I shrugged. "I will say that I'm enjoying it,

though. Jillian? Are you staying here?"

The Corvette chirped as the doors locked and the security system was activated. Swinging the strap from her purse over her neck and shoulder in one fluid motion, Jillian held out a hand and waited for me to pass her Watson's leash. Together, we turned to look at Vance.

"Oh, what the hell. Those two are on to something. I'm willing to bet on it. So, what are you waiting for, Zack? Come on! We have a thief to catch!"

"I would have thought they'd be long gone by now," I said, as the five of us walked companionably down E Street, heading west. "I can only hope these two know what they're doing."

Sherlock looked back at me then, and gave me such a disgusted look, that I had to laugh.

"Wow," Vance laughed. "If a dog had the ability to make a human drop dead from one look, that would have been it."

"It's called corgi stink-eye," I explained. "Thankfully, I don't get it that often, only when Sherlock truly thinks I'm the stupidest thing walking around on two legs."

Sherlock let out a loud snort, as though the little booger had been listening and was letting us know he agreed with the statement.

"What's in this direction?" I wanted to know. "I'll be honest and say that I usually don't come this way. Lentari Cellars is the other way, and if I was going to Cookbook Nook, then I would have turned back there, on 3$^{rd}$ Street."

"We're almost at 3$^{rd}$ and Oregon," Vance mused. He looked at Jillian and shrugged. "There's nothing here but ... look at that. And, we're turning. All right, now what? We're heading south, toward Main Street, guys. We could have driven this."

This time, Jillian and I both laughed. Vance had just been given his very first stink-eye look by a corgi. Properly chastised, our detective friend shoved his hands in his pockets and fell silent.

"What are they putting in here?" I asked, as I looked at the fenced off lot located on the northern side of E Street, at the Oregon Street intersection. "Hopefully, it'll be a restaurant."

"You're always thinking with your stomach," Jillian observed.

Vance hooked a thumb at me. "I'm with him. I think we could use a really good steakhouse."

"We already have one," I argued. "Don't you like Marauder's Grill? They have the best barbecue there."

"Maybe they're relocating?" Vance suggested. "That place never had much in the way of a dining room."

"I'm hoping for a craft store," Jillian said. "Wouldn't that be nice?"

We were only heading south for a few minutes when I sensed the dogs were slowing. Sure enough, the corgis came to a stop, at the intersection of D and Oregon, and turned pensive as they studied the scene. Coming up behind the dogs, I stared at the three-story building and the sprawling parking lot surrounding the building on all sides but the back. In silence, we watched as a group of people, decked out in matching attire, disappeared through the large, arched double-door. Parked just outside this door was a white, customized Ford transit van that had its loading door open. A handicap ramp unfolded from within and lifted a wheelchair, and its occupant, down to the ground.

We were staring at Pomme Acres, PV's one and only nursing home. There, clearly visible in the visitors' parking area just outside the front entrance, was one blue Toyota Prius. Together, the three of us turned to look down at the dogs.

"A nursing home. Oh, you've *got* to be kidding me."

## ELEVEN

How?" I demanded, as I looked down at the dogs. "How do they always do it? I mean, that stupid car could have been anywhere by now. Heck, if the Forces of STUPID were smart, then they should have been on the other side of the county by now. But, where do they decide to stop? At the freakin' nursing home? Where's the logic in that?"

"Let's not jump the gun," Vance cautioned, as we hurried over to the Prius to look through the windows. "Gas prices are still high. Lots of people have these things. But, let's just find out who owns this one, shall we?"

Jillian and I stepped off to the side as Vance phoned the police station with the license plate number. As for Sherlock and Watson, they were paying absolutely no attention to the car. Instead, they were both looking at the nursing facility's front entrance. I tapped Vance on the shoulder and pointed at the dogs. Vance ended the call and pulled us off to the side.

"Okay, listen. This particular Prius is a rental. It's currently showing it was rented in Sacramento ..."

"Ernest," I breathed, as Vance trailed off.

"Exactly what I'm thinking. But, if this is Ernest's car, and we know the guy working with she-who-had-white-hair *isn't* Ernest, then who are we looking for?"

"There were four of them for the scooter chase," I recalled. "Clearly, they must know each other."

"That's what I was thinking," Jillian added. "If they're part of this same organization, and they are all working toward the same goal, then it'd make sense that they'd be willing to work with one another to get the job done."

I pointed at the entrance. "Well? The last time we were here, Sherlock and Watson made quite the stir. Shall we go in and see if anyone at the front desk recognizes Wig Lady?"

"Wig Lady?" Jillian repeated, giggling. "That's the best you can do?"

"We've seen her with three different colors of hair," I pointed out. "What would *you* call her?"

"Wig Lady will do," Vance decided, as he strode toward Pomme Acres' front entrance.

"Just a moment," I called, which drew Vance up

short. "If we know for certain this is a STUPID car, then what are the chances they know we're out here? They could have rented any other car, only they keep using the one Ernest brought up with him from Sacramento. Why is that, do you think?"

"They're acting as though they're on a budget," Jillian began, "but that can't be right, can it?"

"So, if it is, what then?" Vance wanted to know.

I pointed at the car. "That would suggest *this* is their main method of transportation. We don't want to lose it. One of us should stay here, to make sure this thing doesn't go anywhere."

Vance was silent as he considered. After a few moments, he nodded. "All right, I'll buy that. However, Wig Lady had a gun. I'm not about to let you two go in there, unprotected. Hang on. I'm calling for backup."

Less than five minutes later, two officers approached us, only it looked as though they had walked all the way here.

"My patrol car is parked just around the corner," Officer Jones offered, as if he could tell what Jillian and I were thinking. "Detective Samuelson suggested we should keep our cars out of sight, in case someone decides to do something drastic."

"I'm going in with them," Vance reported, as he pointed toward Pomme Acres. "You two are to watch this thing. Don't let anyone get in it. If someone tries, then I want you to detain them. Got it?"

"Keep them here," Officer Jones said, nodding.

"Got it."

"If you need us," the second officer called, as he headed out, "don't be shy."

"Count on it, Officer Stidwell," Vance returned, and then looked at the two of us. "Shall we go see about ruining someone's day?"

"Why, I thought you'd never ask," Jillian exclaimed, as she slipped her arm through mine. Clutching Watson's leash tightly in her hand, she eyed me to make sure Sherlock and I were ready. "After you, Detective."

Vance grinned and nodded. As we approached the entrance, the twin glass sliding doors whooshed open. First and foremost, I detected a strong antiseptic smell, which immediately reminded me of stepping inside a hospital. Just past the entrance doors was a receptionist station, complete with a large, plexiglass window that stretched from the counter all the way up to the ceiling. In the center of the counter was a six-inch wide by four-inch tall opening in the thick glass. I honestly didn't remember seeing this before, and had to wonder if I had just missed it the last time I was here.

"Mr. Anderson!" the receptionist exclaimed, as she finally looked up from her computer screen. "It's so good of you to stop by again! By any chance, did you bring your two adorable dogs? Sherlock and Watson? Are they here?"

A piercing bark made us all jump. The receptionist rose to her feet and practically smooshed her face against the protective glass of her booth in order to see over the counter and inspect the floor. Before she could say anything, I nodded and gave her a sheepish grin.

"That pretty much answers that, doesn't it?"

"Aren't they adorable?"

I nodded. "They are, and they know it. That's the problem."

"Oh, you hush," the receptionist scolded, but did end up giving me a smile. "What can Pomme Acres do for you today, Mr. Anderson?"

I pulled out my phone and brought up the picture I had taken of Wig Lady, from when she had frizzy white hair. "Have you seen her recently? Don't pay any attention to the hair. We're guessing it was a different color when she came in."

"Oh, yes," the receptionist confirmed. "I do remember her. And her hair was most definitely a different color."

"That's her," Vance said, grinning. "Which way did she go?"

"Did she give a name?" Jillian asked.

Vance and I turned to regard the third member of our group.

"What? I'm assuming I get to ask a question or two."

Vance nodded, and promptly took a step back. Jamming my hands in my pockets, I did the same.

"Ms. Cooper! I'm sorry, dear. I didn't see you there. Are you inquiring about the woman who came in about ten minutes ago?"

JEFFREY POOLE

"Ten minutes ago?" I whispered to Vance.

Jillian patted my shoulder and gently pushed me to the side so that she could see the receptionist. "It's good to see you, Mrs. Brannan. By any chance, could you tell me if the driver of the blue Prius out there is the same woman you were just talking about?"

The receptionist's tight gray curls bobbed as she nodded. "My window overlooks the parking lot. I thought it was strange that a hybrid vehicle would come tearing around the corner like that. You'd think that she had just committed a robbery or something."

Jillian let out a small laugh, just as Vance and I grunted with amusement.

"She didn't, did she? Did she hold up a bank?"

"No, ma'am," Vance said. "I just need to find her and ask her a few questions about a case we're working on. It's imperative that we talk to her. Do you know which way she went?"

Mrs. Brannan shook her head. "We get visitors all the time during normal visiting hours. But, I happen to know that, if you want to talk to her, then you're in luck. She has to be still in here, somewhere. All visitors must sign in and out, and she's yet to pass back through."

"What name did she give?" Jillian wanted to know.

Mrs. Brannan reached through the opening in the plexiglass and pulled a clipboard, with an attached pen, toward her. She tapped her finger on

236

the last entry and nodded.

"It says here her name is Julie Moore."

Vance might've shrugged, but both Jillian and I shared a brief look, which didn't go unnoticed by our detective friend.

"What? Do you know her?"

"Only as a thief," I answered, "and that is most definitely not her real name."

"How can you be so sure?" Vance wanted to know.

"Julie Moore?" Jillian quietly repeated. "As in, Julianne Moore? Do you know who she is?"

Vance shook his head. "No, should I?"

"She's a famous red-headed actress," I answered. "It makes me think that Wig Lady might actually be wearing her normal hair for once."

Jillian shrugged. "It's possible."

"Did you ask for identification?" Vance asked, as he turned back to the receptionist.

"It's not a requirement," Mrs. Brannan admitted, "although, to be frank, I'm strongly considering mentioning it to the facility director."

Vance nodded. "Good. Do that. Now, where did she go? Who did she come here to see? Does that clipboard say?"

Mrs. Brannan consulted the guest sign-in sheet a second time. "Liam Gallagher, room #B213."

"How do we find it?" I asked. "Which way?"

In response, Mrs. Brannan pulled a sheet of paper off a shelf next to her work station, circled something, and slid it through the opening.

"We're here. You're looking for the North Wing. Go through that doorway there and follow the hall until it dead ends. Turn left. You'll encounter a nurse's station. Keep going straight, and once you go through another set of double doors, which will be open, you'll be in the North Wing. Mr. Gallagher's room should be near the end of the hall, on the right."

We all thanked the receptionist, with me going so far as to pick up Sherlock so he could stick his snout through the opening and give Mrs. Brannan's hand a few licks. Once we were on our way, Jillian nudged my shoulder.

"Did you notice the name? Liam Gallagher?"

Vance grunted. "Sounds rather Irish, don't you think?"

"Do you think he's involved?" I asked.

"More likely, he's probably related somehow," Vance decided.

"Maybe it's just a coincidence?" Jillian suggested.

We hit the end of the hallway and, as directed, turned left. Another couple of minutes had us emerging into a centralized hub, with hallways headed off in four different directions. At the center of the hub was a large, semi-circular desk. There was a bank of telephones on it, four different computer work stations, and no fewer than six staff members, dressed in identical green surgical scrubs, lounging against the counter. The conversations came to an abrupt stop and, as one, all six

CASE OF THE SHADY SHAMROCK

employees—four women and two men—allowed their gazes to drop to the floor.

"Corgis!" one woman exclaimed.

"How adorable!" another cried.

I sure hope whatever those half-dozen staff members were doing behind the counter wasn't important, because every single one of them came hurrying around the desk to drop into a squat next to the dogs. Sherlock and Watson, as you can probably imagine, slid into *down* positions and rolled over, exposing their furry bellies.

"Really, guys?" I sighed. "We're in the middle of something here. Show a little backbone, would you?"

I was ignored. One of the employees, a young girl in her mid-twenties, looked up at me and smiled.

"You have some adorable dogs."

"The word you're looking for is diva," I clarified, which elicited a round of laughter from everyone present. I pulled out my phone yet again, and showed it to the nurse. "Have you seen this woman lately? Could she have possibly come by this way?"

"What difference does it make?" Vance whispered. "We know which room she visited."

"Allegedly visited," Jillian softly murmured. "It couldn't hurt to get a little confirmation so we know we're on the right track."

"Oh, her," the nurse said, as she rose to her feet. Four of the five other employees did the same.

"Yes, I remember her. She wasn't very nice at all."

I pointed at the hallway directly ahead of us. "Did she go that way?"

The group of nurses all turned to look behind them, as if they didn't believe a hallway was back there.

"Yes," the young nurse said. "Do you need any help? Do you know where you're going?"

I pointed at the hall. "Yep. *That* way. The lady you didn't like? She had something that didn't belong to her. We're thinking she might have stashed it in a room down there."

"Which room?" one of the male nurses asked, growing concerned.

I looked at Jillian. "What was his name, again? Gallagher?"

"Liam Gallagher," my fiancée confirmed.

"You're looking for Mr. Gallagher's room?" another employee asked. This was a woman in her early fifties, and had just emerged from one of the other intersecting corridors. She took one look at our little group and immediately hurried forward so she could place herself in our way. "There's no need to bother Mr. Gallagher now, thank you very much. He's had a rough couple of days, so he needs his rest."

"A rough couple of days?" one of the male nurses repeated, puzzled. "How so? I worked a ten-hour shift yesterday, and every time I looked in on Mr. Gallagher, he was playing solitaire in his bed. He seemed cheerful, not stressed."

"Well, he was," the elderly nurse insisted. "Therefore, we shouldn't … stop right there! Don't you dare go down there!"

Sherlock and Watson had completely ignored this newest obstacle and strolled right past her, as though she had no business trying to impede their progress.

"What seems to be the problem here?" a new voice asked. The voice was strong, firm, and brooked no arguments. "Oh, what's this? Dogs? How wonderful! Our residents will love that!"

"Nurse Hutchens was trying to prevent our visitors from visiting Mr. Gallagher, ma'am," one of the other nurses explained. "I'm just not sure why."

"He's had a rough couple of days," Nurse Hutchens hastily explained.

"No, he hasn't," the head nurse argued. "He's been in low spirits, and a visit from a couple of dogs would be most welcome." She looked over at me and held out a hand. "Sheryl Bates, Director of Nursing."

"Zack Anderson."

A smile appeared on Sheryl's face. "Ah. Lentari Cellars. You make my favorite wine, Mr. Anderson. Now, Nurse Hutchens? Step out of the way. We will be allowing Mr. Anderson and his dogs to visit one of our residents."

With a cry of alarm, Nurse Hutchens turned on her heel and fled down the hall, intent on reaching Mr. Gallagher's room before us. However, before she could make it by the dogs, Sherlock gave one of the nurse's legs a tiny nudge, which was enough to throw her off balance. Down she went, and unfortunately for her, it was a tile floor. Her breath exploded out of her in a whoosh and she painfully rolled onto her back.

"There, there," one of the male nurses said, as they helped Nurse Hutchens off the floor. "Here's a chair. Sit there."

Surprisingly, Nurse Hutchens brushed off the helping hands and tried to get to her feet in an effort to stop us from walking down the hall.

"No! You don't understand! You can't go there!"

"Would this have anything to do with a stolen item being stashed in one of the rooms?" Vance dryly asked, as he approached the nurse and showed his identification. "I do believe I'd like a word with you when this is all said and done."

The nurse let out a cry of alarm and pushed the people crowding around her away. She frantically ran toward the facility's main entrance, just as quickly as she could. Vance casually pulled his cell from his pocket and placed a call.

"Jones? Hey, heads up. There's a woman headed your way, in a hurry. She's ... what? No, listen to me. I'm fairly certain she's involved here. We're going to need to ... what's that? I can't now. Tell us when we're back outside, okay? For now, hold her for questioning, will you? Great. Thanks."

"Bizarre behavior for a nurse," I decided.

"How long has she worked here?" Jillian

wanted to know.

"Less than a year," Sheryl told us, frowning. "And she's involved? With what?"

"A woman came in here," I explained. "She was carrying stolen property. We're pretty sure she stashed it in Liam Gallagher's room."

Sheryl frowned. "Is that so? Come. I'll take you to Mr. Gallagher now."

We followed Sheryl and three of the nurses down the hall and stopped at the right-hand door at the end. Sheryl knocked a few times and then, when she didn't hear anything, she and a second nurse entered. While they presumably checked on the room's occupant, the three of us huddled together.

"What if she's in there?" I asked.

"I doubt it," Vance replied. "I'm thinking she was just looking for a place to stash the chest for a few days, until the hype can die down."

"I wonder if Liam has ever been visited by Ms. Moore before," Jillian wondered.

"I haven't seen her before, if that helps," a young nurse replied, having overheard us.

"I have," another nurse said, holding up a hand.

"How long ago?" I asked. "Any ideas?"

"Sure. I'd say about five days ago."

"Five days?" I repeated, as I turned to look at my two friends. "That's almost the amount of time that a certain something has been in my possession."

"Too coincidental," Vance decided.

Sheryl emerged at Mr. Gallagher's door. "He's ready to receive you. He doesn't know who you are ..." and at this, she lowered his voice, "... but I can tell you that he really doesn't care. He'd love some company."

"Does he like dogs?" I asked.

"I already asked, and yes, he loves dogs."

I looked down at Sherlock and Watson and promptly dropped the leashes. "Go on, you two. Go say hi."

Both corgis took off, as if it was now a race to see who could get there first. However, when we entered the room, we could see that the bed was raised just a little too high for a dog with such short legs. Each of the dogs had reared up, on their squat hind legs, and were giving little jumps, as if they expected to be able to jump up to the bed with minimal effort.

"Mr. Gallagher?" I asked, as I held out a hand. "Zack Anderson. This is my fiancée, Jillian Cooper, and over there, by the television, is Vance Samuelson."

"And who do we have down there?" Liam Gallagher asked, as he propped himself up in his bed and looked down at the dogs. He looked to be in his late sixties, had thinning hair, and was skinny as a rail. He looked down at the dogs and smiled. "Well, aren't they a couple of cuties. What are their names?"

"Sherlock and Watson. With your permission, I can lift them up to your bed, so they can give you a proper introduction."

"Absolutely. I'd love nothing more."

Nodding to Vance, we both picked up the dogs and gently set them on the bed. Sherlock turned to look at me, as if seeking permission to do what I know he wanted to do. I gave each dog a pat on the head and stepped back.

"*Release*, guys."

"Release?" Liam repeated, puzzled. "What would ... oh my! Ack! My dentures! One of my dentures popped out and that one took it!"

Horrified, I looked down at my two dogs and, sure enough, one of them had what looked like half a set of human teeth sticking out of their mouth. Any guesses as to which one had snatched up the dentures the moment it had appeared? I'll give you a hint: his fur was three colors. I faced Sherlock, plastered the sternest look I could muster on my face, and then angrily pointed straight down, which is my way of saying *drop it*. What followed next, it's safe to say, would be talked about for months to come.

Sherlock let out a muffled yip and dropped into a crouch with his head low and rear up high. Anyone familiar with dogs in general will recognize the signs that their furry companion was about to engage in a game of chase. Waggling a finger, I took a step toward Sherlock, intent on scolding him for taking something that wasn't his, but as soon as I moved, I knew it had been a mistake. Sherlock was off, like a shot.

Barking maniacally, and with Watson hot on his nub of a tail, Sherlock leapt off the bed and tore out of the room. He headed down the hall, toward the central nurses' station. I heard exclamations of surprise before a loud yip sounded, which resulted in a mad scrambling of doggie toenails on the tiled floor. After a few moments, Sherlock was back in the doorway, proceeded to bark a challenge, and then took off. I could hear him running down the hall for a second time, letting out a series of challenging barks whenever he saw someone stick their head out of a door to look at him.

"I'm so sorry about this," I managed.

The entire room, including the nurses, Jillian, and Vance, were in hysterics. Even Mr. Gallagher was smiling away as he enjoyed the antics of my two corgis. We noticed the barks were growing progressively louder, and then two canine tornadoes blew into the room. Sherlock had been running so fast that, when he applied the brakes, he slid the remaining five feet across the floor. Now situated at the base of the hospital bed, Sherlock looked up at us and waggled his stump of a tail.

"I love that dog," the head nurse exclaimed. "Omigod, he's so precious!"

"Oh, don't tell him that," I groaned. Steeling myself, I knelt down next to Sherlock and held out my hand. "Fork it over, pal. Those aren't yours."

I maintain he made the noise, only Jillian said she hadn't heard anything. Sherlock looked right at me and made a 'PTUI!' sound. A warm, slobbery item was deposited in my hand. Staring down at the saliva-covered upper half of Mr. Gallagher's dentures, I smiled sheepishly and started to hand them back to its rightful owner. Thankfully, one of the nurses offered to take the false teeth out of my hand, presumably to give the teeth a thorough cleaning.

"Think nothing of it, dear boy," Mr. Gallagher told me, with a sparkle in his eye. "I haven't had this much excitement in months! I like your dogs. You feel free to come around anytime you'd like."

I grinned at the bed's occupant and then pulled out my phone. Bringing up the picture of Julie Moore, and still not being certain that was her actual name, I showed Mr. Gallagher the photograph.

"Do you recognize her, Mr. Gallagher?"

Liam Gallagher automatically pulled on the silver chain around his neck, which I hadn't noticed before, and produced a thin set of eyeglasses. Taking my phone, he studied the photo. I'm also very pleased to say that he began nodding the moment he saw it.

"Her? I've seen her before. I think she's the mother of one of my granddaughters. At least, she said she was."

"Did she give her name?" Jillian asked.

"Moore. Julie Moore, I believe."

"But, you've never seen her before," Vance clarified.

Mr. Gallagher nodded. "That's right. Why? What's the matter?"

"Did she leave anything in here?" I asked, curiously.

Mr. Gallagher pointed at the closed closet door. "As a matter of fact, she did. She had a small, black bag with her. She said I needed to keep its existence quiet."

"May we?" Vance politely inquired, as he reached for the sliding glass closet door, but stopped several inches shy of touching the surface.

"Go ahead," Mr. Gallagher urged.

Vance cautiously slid the door open and, breaking out into a grin, reached inside. Within moments, he had turned around, and there, standing upright before him, was the small, black duffel bag. After a few fist-pumps, Vance carried the bag over to a nearby counter and carefully inspected the bag for damage, which there was none. Slowly unzipping the duffel bag, he spread open the small bag and risked a look inside. Only then did he let out a loud exhale. It was the shamrock chest, and thankfully, it was still very much closed.

"Oh, is that a sight for sore eyes," I breathed.

Vance motioned to the chest and inclined his head. "If you would, Mr. Anderson."

"I would love to, Detective Samuelson," I said, with a grin.

"Property has been reclaimed," Vance noted, in his notebook. "Appears to be intact."

"What is that?" Sheryl wanted to know. "Is it dangerous?"

"Well, we know someone really wants it," Vance told the head nurse. "As for what it is, no, it's not dangerous. At least, if it contains what we think it does, then it isn't."

"What do you think it contains?" one nurse asked.

I shrugged, as I slid the chest under my arm. "Oh, nothing really. We suspect this thing contains the stolen crown jewels from Ireland."

As we thanked Liam Gallagher, promising to bring the dogs back sometime later in the week so that all the residents would be able to meet them, we heard several of the nurses chatting excitedly among themselves. Should I have revealed what we suspected was in the chest? Probably not. Then again, what did it matter? We weren't keeping them. In fact, if luck went our way, I was hoping to make a second call to my friend in Ireland later tonight.

On the way back to Pomme Acres' main entrance, Vance, Jillian, and I were all chatting among ourselves, laughing, cracking jokes, and giving the dogs friendly scratches. We had stopped by several rooms on the way out, plus— at Sheryl's request—swung by the residents' common area to say hello. The dogs were a hit. Resident faces lit up with delight as each of the corgis made a point to try and make as many new friends as possible. Our good mood, though, disappeared as we emerged outside.

Three police cars were visible, and three officers were slowly walking back and forth in front of the nursing facility. A fourth had stopped to talk with one of the residents after they had walked out, blinking in the bright sunshine, like a bear emerging from hibernation. Where had the other officers come from? And, more importantly, why?

Officer Jones approached and nodded his head. Vance promptly took the lead of our procession and nodded back.

"Jones? What's going on? Why'd you call for backup?"

"Standard procedure," Officer Jones explained, "when you take more than one person into custody."

"You took someone else into custody?" I asked, surprised. "Who?"

Jones pointed at the closest squad car. I could see someone was sitting in the backseat. However, the person was turned away from me and I couldn't tell who it was. That was when the prisoner suddenly whipped their head around, and I saw a flash of red.

"Well, well," I grinned, as I gave a thumbs-up to Officer Jones, "if it isn't Ms. Julie Moore. Hey there! We were wondering about you!"

From the look of disgust and hatred that appeared on Ms. Moore's face, I can only imagine that, if she hadn't been handcuffed, she would have given us the one-finger salute. Sitting in the next car over? One weepy Nurse Hutchens. She took one look at us and immediately turned away. Once the incarcerated nurse was looking away from me, I finally was able to get a good look at her. Same high cheekbones, same nose, and the same hair color, although, to be fair, Nurse Hutchens' was significantly grayer. I found that odd, seeing how the two of them looked to be about the same age.

"Are they related?" Jillian asked, correctly guessing what I had been thinking.

I shrugged. "I kinda think they could be. However, what are the odds of that happening? We were told the person who rented this car did so from Sacramento."

"Ernest was from Sacramento," Jillian recalled, "but I don't think we ever heard where Julie Moore was from. Could she have been here in Pomme Valley?"

"Proof positive that the Forces of STUPID are everywhere," I grinned.

Jillian swatted my arm. "That's not what I meant, but I understand the inference. Vance? Do you need us for anything more?"

Vance shook his head. "I don't believe so. You guys taking off?"

I looked down at the chest and nodded. "Yeah, I think so. We need to figure out if this thing contains what we *think* it contains."

"Keep me posted, pal," Vance called, as we headed to our borrowed Corvette.

"Will do."

Thirty minutes later, after we returned Dottie's car to her and reclaimed the Ruxton, the two of us were sitting comfortably on the couch in my living room. With our chaperones present, namely, the two ever-observant corgis, Jillian and I turned our attention to the chest.

"You ready for this?" I inquired.

Jillian nodded. "I'm so excited! Do you really think we're about to find the missing Irish Crown Jewels?"

"I sure hope so. My friend in Cork would owe me big if they were. All right. Do you remember what the first step is?"

Jillian gazed at the box. "The corner and the thistle. Those were the two areas Sherlock touched with his nose."

I scooted closer to the shamrock chest. "All right. Here goes the corner." I gave the aforementioned corner a slight twist. "And ... now the thistle." I pressed the stem. "Now what?"

"Let's see what else moves," Jillian said, as she began touching various areas. "See? I was right. The circle around the cross? It no longer moves!"

"What about the sun or the horses?" I asked, as I recalled several of the other pieces that had previously been moveable. "Let me give them a try. Well, the sun is out. Let me try the horses. No, they're out, too."

"How does this help us?"

"We need to figure out what the second step is," Jillian answered, as her delicate hands started poking and prodding the chest in several places at once. "Something, somewhere on this chest, should now be able to be moved. We have to find out what it is."

After about ten minutes of exploring, and at the point when I was ready to lower the chest down so that Sherlock could take a look, Jillian found the answer: the fish. There was a tiny pond, on the back of the chest and there, leaping out of the water, was the fish. It hadn't budged before. Now? It was pushable, er, *pressable*, like a button. You'd never know I was a full-time writer, huh?

"That's step two!" Jillian exclaimed with excitement. "Where's your notebook, Zachary? I want to write this down."

In this manner, the two of us uncovered a series of fourteen—yes, you read that right—steps, using just about every decoration there was on the chest. There were even a few steps that had us using previously used pieces. After the fourteenth step had been completed, which, appropriately enough, was the same movable shamrock petal, we heard a loud click. The top portion of the chest trembled, and just like that, a lid appeared, and it was *loose*!

"I'm so nervous!" Jillian cried, as we both leaned forward to stare at the chest.

"Would you allow me?" I offered, as I positioned my hands on either side of the lid, to better open the blasted thing.

"Please do."

My guess was that the chest hadn't been opened since it had originally been stolen, which would have been over 110 years ago. Would it open? Would I need to whip out a can of WD-40? However, the lid noiselessly lifted, revealing a plush, black velvet-lined interior. There was a cinched bag, made up of the same velvet material as the inside of the chest, nestled in the center. Carefully, with hands that were starting to tremble, I opened the pouch and slowly let the contents slide into my hand. Two objects, which I later learned were created in 1831 for the Sovereign and Grand Master of the Order of Saint Patrick, and hadn't seen the light of day since at least 1907, appeared: a heavily jeweled star and diamond-encrusted badge regalia.

The long lost Irish Crown Jewels had been found at last!

## EPILOGUE

D o you have any idea what this means? To think, after all these years, Ireland's greatest mystery has been solved! And it's all thanks to you, my friend."

"Oh, no you don't, Michael. I really didn't have much to do with it, so I can't claim the credit."

"Oh? Who, then? Your lovely fiancée?"

"Uh, er, no. Well, I mean, she helped."

"If not you, or your fiancée, then who was directly involved? Your local constabulary?"

"I have a good friend, Vance Samuelson, who is a detective with the, um, constabulary, and he *did* help, but believe it or not, he wasn't directly responsible, either."

"Then who? Do enlighten me."

"Oh, you're gonna laugh. All right. You can thank Sherlock and Watson. Their help was invaluable, not only in being able to open the silver shamrock chest, but also with tracking it down after it had been stolen."

"The chest had been stolen?" Michael O'Connell, former Lord Mayor of Cork, exclaimed.

"Twice, actually," I confirmed. "Sherlock and Watson tracked it down, both times."

"Are they available to speak on the phone?" Michael formally asked. "I'd like to personally thank them for their actions."

"Hmm. Tell you what. I can put the call on speakerphone. They're both here with me right now."

"That would be most welcome, Zachary. Are they listening?"

I looked down at the dogs and grinned. Yes, both Sherlock and Watson were in the room with me, so I hadn't been lying, but no, they most certainly were not listening. Why? They were too busy chewing on their latest treats, given to them by Vance. And what might those treats be? Just their most favorite ingredient in the whole wide world, which—coincidentally—I found utterly disgusting: pizzle sticks. If you have to ask what those are, then I encourage you to look them up on Google. There's a reason why they are a favorite among dogs.

*Blech.*

"They're here, Michael, but I am sorry to say they really aren't paying too much attention. In fact, they're both ignoring me at the moment.

They're more interested in their pizzle sticks my detective friend gave them."

There was a very noticeable silence as Michael, no doubt, digested this bit of information. Finally, after a few moments had passed, I heard him clear his throat.

"Are Sherlock and Watson canines?"

"They are," I confirmed. "Two Pembroke Welsh Corgis."

"You're telling me," Michael slowly began, using that wonderful Irish lilt I admired so much, "that the return of the Irish Crown Jewels can be attributed to two corgis? Oh, Her Majesty the Queen is going to love this!"

It was my turn to go speechless.

"You're, um, not going to tell that to the actual queen, are you? Forgive my ignorance, but Ireland is no longer under the queen's rule, right?"

"Ireland is a constitutional republic," Michael explained. "We have a president, just like you. But, that doesn't mean our president is not on good speaking terms with the Queen of England. In fact, I do believe he's on the phone with her right now."

"About ...?"

"You, of course. I'm notifying my friend, who is a current member of the House of Parliament, about your two corgis via text message. He'll pass that information along, just as he passed the news of the recovery to the President just a few moments ago."

"You broke the news via text?" I incredulously

asked.

"Modern technology, Zachary. As you Americans would say, 'you gotta love it'! Oh, look at that. He's responding."

"Uh, er, your friend from Parliament? What did he say?"

"It's just as I thought. The President wishes to thank you personally. And, I have to say, word has been sent to the Queen."

I looked down at my dogs, just as Sherlock looked up. We locked eyes on each other and seemingly entered a staring contest. Naturally, I lost. Sherlock cocked his head, as if he had noticed something amiss, and then returned to his revolting treat. They were both going to get a number of dog bones tonight, only I wish it hadn't been a bag full of *those*. The smell of those chews was making me sick to my stomach. Then again, it might also have something to do with the Queen of England, the world's most famous lover of corgis, learning about Sherlock and Watson. Holy crap on a cracker! I have no idea what to say about that.

"How should I get these things back to you?" I asked. "I mean, I really don't trust dropping the jewels off at the nearest shipping facility and hope they make it there. I wouldn't trust a private courier either. I'd like to suggest a personal visit, to escort them home, so to speak, but that's an awful long way to go."

"I asked that question a few moments ago, too," Michael informed me. "It has been decided that we will send someone to *you*, if that is acceptable."

"You're sending someone all the way from Ireland, to Pomme Valley? That's an awful long trip. I wouldn't want to be the one responsible for having to cover all those miles."

"We've had no fewer than three dozen applicants volunteer to have the honor of escorting the Irish Crown Jewels home."

"But … I just broke the news to you about their recovery ten minutes ago! How could there be so many people who know about it?"

"News travels fast in the digital age," Michael patiently explained. "Plus, I've been bragging that I'm currently negotiating to have the jewels returned to us. Whoever we select should be at your doorstep in less than three days. I am sorry I have to ask you to hold on to the jewels a few days longer. It must be uncomfortable for you."

"What is?" I wanted to know.

"To have something that valuable in your possession."

"Believe it or not, it hasn't been the priciest."

"Oh?"

"Ever hear of the *Czarina's Tear*?"

"The famous Russian garnet? Of course."

"I've held it in my hands. I'm currently engaged to its owner."

"That's why Pomme Valley is so familiar to me. I've seen it on the telly!"

"The telly. I love it. Anyway, I can keep it safe.

Been doing that all week."

Jillian chose that time to walk into my study. Not realizing I was in the middle of a phone call, she companionably rested a hip on the corner of my desk and was ready to ask me something when I was given some rather startling news.

"I just got word," Michael reported, drawing an embarrassed look from Jillian. She tried to leave, but I snatched her hand and pulled her to my side. "Her Majesty has been informed of your involvement, and that of your two dogs, and has requested a meeting."

Jillian's eyebrows shot up. "The Queen of England?"

"Who's there?" Michael asked, having overheard Jillian's question.

"Michael O'Connell, meet Jillian Cooper, my fiancée. She just walked into the room. Jillian, this is a friend of mine who helped with some research for one of my books a while back. At the time, he was Lord Mayor of Cork. I do believe he's considering running for office again."

"This is the friend you were talking about, isn't it?" Jillian asked. She leaned over my desk. "Michael, you live in Ireland? Oh, how wonderful!"

"Jillian has never been," I explained to my friend. "She and I are planning on spending our honeymoon there.

"A finer country you will never see," Michael announced, deepening his voice and deliberately thickening his accent. "You'll love it here, Ms.

Cooper."

"I can't wait to see it," Jillian returned. "Now, what about the queen?"

"Her Majesty has learned of your two corgis' involvement in the return of the stolen Irish Crown Jewels," Michael explained. "She has requested a meeting. Both she and our illustrious president are devising a way to thank you both."

"The queen and the president are *what*?" I slowly repeated.

"Didn't I mention it before? Dear me, I do believe it must have slipped my mind. At any rate, once your reward has been determined, then I'll be reaching out to you, I'm sure."

"No reward is ..." I began, but was flat-out ignored.

"We'll be in touch, Zachary. It was good to meet you, Ms. Cooper."

"Likewise, Michael," Jillian returned.

My cell darkened once the call had been terminated. Jillian and I looked at each other, and then we both burst out in nervous laughter. However, before either of us could say anything, Jillian's phone chimed once, signaling an incoming text message. Still smiling, she pulled her phone from her pocket and glanced at the display. Before I knew what was happening, Jillian's lovely face was frowning and her head tilted, as if she had just received a bit of puzzling news.

"What is it?" I asked. "Did your mother contact you again with some silly story about your dad?"

Jillian slowly handed me her phone. There, on the display, was the message, and it consisted of just a couple of sentences:

JUST HEARD THE NEWS, WELL DONE. KNEW SENDING IT TO Z WAS RIGHT DECISION. WILL TALK LATER, HAVE TO GO.

"What am I looking at?" I wanted to know. "Are they talking about the chest? And whoever that is, they sent me the flippin' thing?"

Jillian nodded, still at a loss for words.

"Who sent that message?" I asked.

"Zachary, this message is from Joshua. My brother sent you that chest!"

# AUTHOR'S NOTE

Thank you for reading the latest novel in my growing Corgi Case Files cozy mystery series. I have a great time writing these adventures, and I can only hope you enjoy reading them as much as I enjoy writing 'em. I have a few disclaimers to throw out there, so please, bear with me for a few moments.

Like me, before I started this book, I'll bet most of you have never heard of the Irish Crown Jewels. When I went searching for something I could use for the contents of the shamrock chest, I stumbled upon Ireland's greatest mystery, and voila! The story started to write itself.

If you couldn't tell, both my wife and I loved visiting Ireland. We've been wanting to travel to the Emerald Isle for a number of years now, so when our 20th anniversary arrived last year, we treated ourselves to a cruise around the British Isles. If you've never been, then please trust me. It's worth a trip. The Blarney Woollen shop in Cork is worth the trip alone just for their selection of Waterford crystal.

Up next for Zack and the gang will be the Case of the Ragin' Cajun, as Zack is finally talked into attending a book signing at a massive book fair in New Orleans. Since his recent book about Ireland, with Tori as the inspiration for the protagonist, is garnering all kinds of publicity, Vance and Tori have been invited, too. Well, when they get there, it's not hard to believe things go awry.

Looking for something else to read while you wait for Zack and the dogs to return? Look no further! I heartily recommend:

- The Samantha Sweet mysteries, by Connie Shelton
- The Ben Pecos mysteries, by Susan Slater
- A little more intense, I know, but I do enjoy the Agent Pendergast series, by Preston & Child

Finally, if you enjoyed the story, please consider leaving a review wherever you purchased the book. Authors love reviews, and the more reviews they can get, the easier they can be found at the large online retailers.
Until next time!

J.
November, 2020

**THE CORGI CASE FILES SERIES**
*Available in e-book and paperback*

*If you enjoy Epic Fantasy, check out Jeff's other series:*
Pirates of Perz
Tales of Lentari
Bakkian Chronicles

Made in the USA
Las Vegas, NV
12 August 2023

76000235R10163